THE CASE FOR
DEFINITE
CERTAINTY

THE CASE OF THE
DEAD
CERTAINTY

KEL RICHARDS

Hodder & Stoughton

A Hodder & Stoughton Book

Published in Australia and New Zealand in 1995
by Hodder Headline Australia Pty Limited
(A member of the Hodder Headline Group)
10–16 South Street, Rydalmere NSW 2116

National Library of Australia
Cataloguing-in-Publication data

Richards, Kel. 1946–
    The case of the dead certainty.

    ISBN 0 340 62257 1.

    I. Title.

A823.3

Typeset in Australia by DOCUPRO, Sydney
Printed in Australia by Griffin Paperbacks

For
James W. Sire

AUTHOR'S NOTE

Just as Shakespeare in modern dress is still Shakespeare, so history in modern dress is still history. Despite the pizzas, guns, cars and telephones this fictional detective story is based on a solid, historical reality of the first century AD — namely, the early years of the Christian church.

For old friends who have read Ben Bartholomew's previously published adventures a word of explanation: the events of this story fall in between *The Case of the Damascus Dagger* and *The Case of the Secret Assassin*, occurring shortly after the former and more than twenty years before the latter.

ACKNOWLEDGEMENT

All direct Biblical quotations in this story are taken with permission from *The Living Bible: A thought-for-thought paraphrase* by Kenneth N. Taylor, and *The Message: The New Testament in contemporary English*, a translation by Eugene H. Peterson.

CHAPTER 1

'It's a backward step,' I said firmly.

'It's a backward step that will pay us money,' insisted Rachel.

'It's a matter of principle.'

'It's a matter of the rent!'

'Besides which...I might fail.'

'You won't. It's a missing persons case. When you were a private detective you were very good at missing persons cases.'

'But I'm not a private eye any longer! It's not a suitable job for a married man. That's why I dusted off my old law degree and hung a brass plate beside the front door saying *Ben Bartholomew, Counsellor-at-Law.*'

'And so far not a lot of people have required your counsel,' said Rachel tartly.

'Give it time, give it time.'

'That's not what the landlord says. "Give me money, give me money," that's what he says!'

'So things have been slow...'

'Any slower and we would have been arrested for loitering!'

'Rachel...' I pleaded.

'She's right!' boomed a voice from the next room. 'You should listen to your wife, Benjamin!'

'Momma, you've been listening,' I snapped.

'Of course I've been listening,' said Momma as

she pushed open the kitchen door and bustled into our tiny sitting-room. 'What's the point of my coming all the way from Jerusalem to visit my son and my daughter-in-law if I don't listen?'

'Tell him to be sensible, Momma,' urged Rachel.

'I'm telling him already. But do you think he'll listen? For thirty-seven years he hasn't listened; you imagine he'll start now?'

'Momma, be reasonable,' I pleaded.

'Reasonable? What's to be reasonable about? Here you are living in a pokey little apartment above a pokey little office in Caesarea with no money coming in. I say "Take the money," Rachel says "Take the money," and you say we're not being reasonable? Benjamin, take a look in your shaving mirror — there's a most unreasonable man in there!'

'That's not fair! All I'm saying is that a married man should have a respectable profession. Rachel, do you want me slinking around back-alleys by night?'

'Do I want you starving in your office by day?' answered Rachel with a shrug of her shoulders. 'Because that appears to be the choice we have.'

I was about to reply when the door-bell to the office downstairs chimed.

'That will be Joe,' said Rachel, 'I'll go and let him in. You brush those crumbs off your jacket and come down in a minute. And at least listen to what he has to say before you tell him "No." '

'She's a good wife you have there, Benjamin,' said Momma as Rachel disappeared downstairs. 'You should listen to her — a mother knows these things.'

'Yes, Momma,' I said wearily, not wanting another argument.

'In wanting to be a successful lawyer by yesterday you are putting the chariot entirely before the horses,

Benjamin. Get some money coming in, decorate your little apartment, make it a nice little home and *then* worry about what profession you're in.'

'That's not what you used to say, Momma, when I was a full time PI in Jerusalem!'

'I want that you and Rachel should be happy, my son. You can't live on hugs and kisses; you have to eat occasionally.'

'Momma...' I began.

'You go downstairs now,' interrupted Momma. 'Your client will be waiting.'

And just as I've been doing for the past thirty-seven years — I did like Momma told me.

At the foot of the stairs I turned right and stepped into the office that was almost over-filled by one desk, two chairs, and a small book-case full of second-hand law books.

'Ben, you know Mr Jacobson, don't you?' said Rachel, making the unnecessary introductions.

Of course I knew Joe Jacobson: Rachel and I saw Joe and his family every week at synagogue.

'Sit down, Joe,' I said, waving him back into the client's chair that he had half-risen out of when I entered. I edged my way around the desk and sat down in the cracked leather of my second-hand executive swivel-chair. As always, my momentum spun the chair around so that I found myself facing the back wall of the office. I spun back again.

'Will you take my case, Ben?' said Joe, leaning forward across the desk, his eyes pleading even more heavily than his voice. Beneath a bald scalp, with just an untidy fringe of brown hair, Joe had a thin, narrow face. Worry made it look somehow narrower, and sharper.

Normally a fastidious dresser, tonight Joe's cloak

was falling off his shoulders, and his fine linen tunic was streaked with dust.

'Will you find Abigail for me, Ben?'

Immediately behind him Rachel was standing nodding a vigorous "yes."

'Joe,' I hesitated, 'I'm not sure. I'm not in the private eye business anymore...'

'Please, Ben. I know your reputation. When it comes to missing persons you're the best. And Hannah and I are worried sick.'

'Tell me about it, Joe,' I said with a heavy sigh. I could see that with Rachel (and Momma!) pushing, and Joe pulling, I wasn't about to get out of this.

'Like I told you on the telephone, Abigail's been missing for four days now. She's only seventeen years of age. She's never done anything like this before. It's out of character. Her mother and I, we...well, we...just don't know what to do.'

'Have you reported her disappearance to the authorities?'

'Oh, yes! When she didn't come home on Tuesday night. I went up to the palace and talked to a Roman army officer. He said he'd have the city watch keep their eyes open for her. But he didn't offer any hope.'

'Have you searched for her yourself?'

'Of course! Of course! Hannah and I have visited all her friends. And all our friends. Everywhere we could think of. Anywhere she might go.'

'And no one's seen her?'

He gave a helpless shrug, and the cloak slipped even further off his shoulders. 'Not since Tuesday morning,' he said. 'Do you think she's all right, Ben? What could have happened to her?'

'Does she have any history of medical problems?'

'Medical problems?' said Joe. 'What sort of medical problems?'

'Dizzy spells, fainting fits, memory loss — anything that might have caused her disappearance.'

'Oh, I see what you mean. No, she has no history of anything of that sort. Is that what you think happened, Ben? Do you think she's ill somewhere?'

'Do you have a photograph of her, Joe?'

'Sure, sure, I brought one with me.'

As he spoke he fished into his top pocket and produced a small snapshot of a pretty girl with dark, shoulder-length hair. Her prettiness was emphasised by the contrast between the paleness of her skin and the darkness of her deep, brown eyes. In the picture she was wearing a blue robe with very little decoration, just some embroidery around the yoke. I vaguely remembered her from synagogue: a quiet, shy girl. Even in the photo she looked shy — as if she was flinching away from the camera.

'Can I keep this?' I asked.

'Yes, of course.'

'What sort of a girl is Abigail, Joe? Describe her to me.'

'She's like that,' he replied, gesturing at the snapshot on my desk and looking puzzled.

'I mean character, Joe,' I explained. 'Personality — what is she like?'

'Well, she's quiet and studious. Not one of your crazy adolescents, you understand?'

I nodded.

'Maybe she's a bit spoiled. She's an only child, you know. And Hannah and I...well, we've indulged her a bit, I guess. But she's a *nice* girl. People meet her, they like her.'

'Does she have many friends? Hobbies? Interests?'

'Not a lot of friends. She's quiet, like I said. She reads a lot. As for interests, well, just lately she's become very interested in religion.'

'How interested? Obsessed?'

'Oh, no! I wouldn't say that. She's very sceptical, you know. She takes a lot of convincing. She asks questions, and challenges everything. At college they always said she's a very bright girl. You know, high IQ, mature for her age, that sort of thing.'

'I understand. So this religious kick, when did it begin?'

'Maybe a month ago, maybe a little more. She started visiting the temples of Caesarea. You know, going from temple to temple, seeing what each one had to offer.'

'Temples?' My eyebrows shot up as I spoke. 'Pagan temples? A good Jewish girl like Abigail has been visiting pagan temples?'

'Yeah, well. She got interested and I didn't really approve (which I told her) but she wanted to, and so she did.'

'I get the impression she pretty much does what she likes, Joe — that right?'

'Like I said, she's an only child, so we spoil her a little. Is that a crime?'

'Keep your toga on, no need to get upset. Now, when was the last time you saw her?'

'Tuesday morning. She helped to clean up the breakfast things and then she left the house.'

'Did she say where she was going?'

'She said to the public library.'

'Did you believe her?'

'Sure, I believed her. She's a reader.'

'And you haven't seen her since then?'

Joe Jacobson shook his head and his eyes glistened, but he held back the tears.

'Will you take the case, Ben?' he asked.

'I'll take the case. I'll find Abigail for you, Joe. Don't you worry, I'll find her.'

'So…when and where do you start?' asked Joe.

'Right now,' I replied.

'Yes,' said Rachel, 'it's urgent. We'll begin at once.'

'What's this "we" business?' I asked.

'This is *our* case, darling,' said my beautiful dark-haired wife, 'and we'll work on it together.'

'I'm not so sure…' I began.

'I'll leave you two to sort this out,' interrupted Joe. 'Call me if you have any more questions. By the way, what do you charge for this sort of work?'

'A hundred denariis a day,' I said.

'Plus expenses,' added Rachel.

'I'll pay anything to get my daughter back,' said Joe. 'Spend whatever you need to. I'll go back home to Hannah now and tell her that you're taking our case. She'll be very relieved.'

After he had managed to squeeze out of the client's chair and edge his way out of my tiny office I turned to Rachel. She was wearing the pale blue tunic that women usually wear — much like the one Abigail was wearing in the snapshot. But there the resemblance ended. Where Abigail looked pale, and her expression hesitant, Rachel's face was shining with enthusiasm and intelligence. Apart from a fringe on her forehead, her long hair was pulled back and held in place by beautiful ivory combs. She looked far too lovely to get involved in a criminal investigation.

'What's this business about "our case," Rachel my

love? I thought I was the private investigator in the family.'

'Well, it's a bigger family now. You're a married man, so that means you're part of a team of two.'

'Not a team of two detectives, I'm not! No way! The work is grubby and the work is dangerous.'

'All the more reason why I should come along to keep an eye on you,' insisted Rachel with the sweetest smile.

'I don't understand, honey,' I said, running my hand through the remains of my hair. 'I thought you hated detective work. I thought you were pleased when I decided to return to the law.'

'I do. And I am. But this is the only work available, so this is the work you must do. And if you must do it, so must I.'

'That doesn't follow,' I replied, determined to put my sandal down firmly on this nonsense.

'We agreed,' said Rachel gently, slipping up close to me and putting her arm around my waist, 'that I would work as your secretary, didn't we?'

'Well…take some dictation then!' I said, trying hard not to waver.

'And more than just a secretary — a personal assistant, we said.'

'Ah…hmmm…yes, we did say that.'

'So, if you are a detective again — however briefly — then I am, for the time being at least, an assistant detective.'

At that point she kissed me, and I lost the argument.

'So…where does our investigation begin?' asked Rachel some time later, when the brain took over from the hormones again.

'At the Jacobson house,' I replied, gathering my thoughts. 'We need to search Abigail's room.'

CHAPTER 2

Caesarea is a typical Roman city in many ways: broad, straight main streets, lots of palaces and public buildings, an enormous amphitheatre, and in the middle a huge temple dedicated to Caesar and Rome and containing vast statues of the emperor. The city had been built by Herod the Great and named in grovelling honour of Caesar Augustus. I'll never know why Herod didn't go all the way and just call the place 'May-I-Lick-Your-Boots-Please-And-Call-You-Sir'!

All this Roman neatness and order was rather ruined by the myriad of pagan temples that had sprung up on every street corner, and by the hundreds of ramshackle market stalls that appeared in the forum, the large, open square in the heart of the city.

As a major port, and a trading post on the caravan route between Tyre and Egypt, Caesarea was a bustling commercial centre filled with every imaginable nationality. Romans, Greeks, Jews, Egyptians, dark-skinned Africans, fair-skinned Britons, and argumentative Gauls: they all could be found on the streets of the city.

The city has that distinctive aroma that only port cities have, and then only when the wind is blowing in from the sea: a delicate mixture of salt-spray and dead fish. It was the sort of smell that gave your nostrils a vigorous work-out for the day.

As we passed under one of the arches of the city's main aqueduct I became aware of the sand under our feet. Whenever there was an on-shore breeze, sand blew up from the waterfront and became a thin layer that crunched under leather sandals and wooden wheels.

We turned away from the public buildings, the wharves and the warehouses, towards the north side of Caesarea, where the Jacobsons' villa stood, in the residential quarter favoured by wealthy merchants.

'So, we are going to look in Abigail's room?' asked Rachel as we walked.

'That's right.'

'And what are we looking for?'

'I don't know, sweetheart. I never do know at the start of a case. Anything that will give us a hint as to what was on her mind in the hours, or days, before she disappeared.'

The Jacobson dwelling turned out to be a typical Roman villa, the sort of standard-plan affair that contract builders knock up for anyone who can shell out the shekels. A windowless white wall faced the street — providing privacy for the family, who would spend much of their time in the central courtyard and the rooms opening off it. The wall was broken only by double wooden doors flanked by mock-Grecian pillars. I knocked and waited.

A porter admitted us, and a maid showed us through into the atrium, where she asked us to take a seat.

A moment later Joe appeared with his wife, Hannah, at his side. Hannah was red-eyed from crying, her once dark hair, now streaked with grey, hung in untidy strands over her shoulders and down her back. She dabbed at her eyes with a corner of her shawl. The women hugged each other and Rachel patted Hannah's shoulder, but didn't say anything.

'We've come to see Abigail's room,' I explained to Joe while the women were doing their grappling number, 'to see if we can pick up any clues that you and Hannah might have missed.'

'Sure,' he said, 'this way.'

He led us across the atrium to one of the bedrooms at the back of the house.

'This is Abi's room,' said Joe, looking somewhat moist-eyed himself.

'Why don't you leave Rachel and me to have a look around by ourselves,' I suggested. 'We'll check with you before we leave.'

'Sure. Come along, Hannah, leave these people to do their job.'

I shut the door behind them and glanced around.

'Not a typical teenager's room,' commented Rachel.

'In what way?' I asked.

'For a start it's neat and tidy.'

'Yeah, I see what you mean. I can actually see the floor!'

'That's right. For a typical seventeen-year-old we should be knee-deep in robes, sandals, cloaks and shawls that have been worn once and then dropped in the middle of the room.'

'And another thing,' I added, 'no pin-up pictures of gorgeous gladiators on the walls.'

'That's right!' agreed Rachel. 'I had hunks all over my walls when I was seventeen.'

'Oh, did you just? This is something I hadn't heard before.'

'It's a bit late to be jealous now, Ben darling.'

Abigail Jacobson's room had plain white washed

walls and was plainly furnished with one wooden bed, one desk, one chair, and one chest which, when opened, proved to contain neatly folded robes and precisely stacked sandals.

'All very Spartan,' I commented.

'Yes, I do detect a Greek influence in the decorating,' said Rachel.

The desk was piled high with book-scrolls, but again arranged in a very neat and symmetrical fashion.

On the right-hand side of the desk was a jotting pad of papyrus with a writing stylus and bottle of ink.

'And the only thing *that* demonstrates,' I said, indicating the writing materials, 'is that she was right-handed.'

I hunted through the scrolls and found them to be a mixture of gnostic mystical rubbish and high-brow philosophical waffle. There was the *Cosmology* of Hermes Trismegistos, Pythagoras on *The Triangulation of Reality*, Aristotle's *Prior and Posterior Analytics*, and several others.

'You check out her clothes,' I suggested. 'I want to find some of her own notes and jottings if I can.'

But I couldn't. An hour of solid searching produced a zero that looked as neat as the room.

'But she must have made notes.'

'So where are they then?' asked Rachel. 'Could she have burnt them?'

'Why write something down, just to burn it? What can you tell me about the girl's clothes?'

'Nothing, except for the fact that there doesn't appear to be much missing.'

'So, if she didn't pack a trunk full of clothes then

perhaps — and I stress *perhaps* — she didn't intend to vanish.'

Then we tried pulling the bed apart and searching through the bed linen. The result? Nothing, except clean, neat sheets and pillowcases.

'But she must have made some notes if she did all this reading and studying,' I muttered.

'Perhaps she took her notes with her?' proposed Rachel.

'Yeah...maybe. Hang on! I've just thought of something!'

And with those words I began unwinding Abigail's book-scrolls all over the floor.

'Ben! You're making a terrible mess!'

'So report me to the sanitation department already!' I snapped as I kept on unrolling. A dozen scrolls later, I hit the jackpot.

'Eureka!'

'Don't talk Greek to me,' complained Rachel, her pretty lips pouting in a pretence of anger.

'Look, look, here's what I was searching for.'

As I spoke, a small slip of notepaper came fluttering out onto the floor. It had been tightly wound into the very centre of one of the book-scrolls.

'How do you know this is important?'

'Because, Rachel my love, it was hidden. People only hide important notes.'

I unfolded the papyrus and found it filled with small neat writing. Across the top was an underlined heading: SEARCHING FOR TRUTH. Underneath was a list of temples:

SEARCHING FOR THE TRUTH

The Temple of the Great Clockmaker

The Temple that Matters

The Nothingness Temple

The Temple of the Golden Eye

The One Temple

The Inner Temple

The haunted Temple

'So what does the note amount to?' asked Rachel.

'The key, sweetheart,' I replied, 'the key to the mystery.'

CHAPTER 3

'Do you recognise the names of the temples on that list?' asked Rachel.

'Not all of them,' I said. 'I know of The Clockmaker (everyone knows that), and The Inner Temple is the one that's been in the news lately, but the others I'll need to check up on.'

'Where can you do that?'

'A newspaperman might know. I'll check with Laconicus.'

'*We* will check with Laconicus — this is a detective partnership, remember.'

'I have another job for you, Rachel.'

'And what might that be?'

'While I'm in the newspaper office you call into the city library. Take this snapshot of Abigail with you. See if any of the staff recognise her and, particularly, find out if anyone remembers seeing her in the library on Tuesday morning. Meanwhile, I'll run this list of temples by my favourite drunken hack, Petronius Laconicus, and see if the names mean anything to him.'

'Right, chief,' she replied, giving me a mock salute.

'This room has nothing more to tell us, I suspect,' I said, looking around. 'So let's get moving.'

'First,' said Rachel, 'we should tidy up the mess

we made, and put the room back into the apple-pie order in which we found it.'

'I'm a detective, not a housemaid,' I began to argue. Then Rachel flashed a look at me with those beautiful brown eyes of hers, a look that could kill an argument stone-dead at a hundred paces.

We tidied the room.

Before we left the Jacobson house I needed to speak to Joe and Hannah. We found them waiting in the atrium.

'We've finished in Abigail's room,' I explained, 'but I have one question: are any of your daughter's things missing — as far as you can tell?'

'No, I don't think so,' answered Hannah.

'Not even clothes?' I persisted.

'Only the clothes she was wearing. As far as I can tell, the rest of my daughter's belongings are still there.'

In front of the house, Rachel and I separated. She headed up the hill towards the administrative district, where the palaces and public buildings were to be found. I headed towards the docks, where the offices of Caesarea's daily newspaper, the *Acta Diurna*, were located.

I shouldered my way through the busy late-afternoon crowds, jostling the other pedestrians, and dodging the donkeys, camels, carts and chariots.

In front of the newspaper's harbourside building was a wharf piled high with giant rolls of papyrus, and tied up at the wharf was an Egyptian galley from which more rolls were being unloaded. I ducked out of the blazing sunshine into the cool interior of the building. The ground floor was occupied by hundreds of slave-scribes copying the evening edition of the paper. A broad staircase led me to the first floor, where the journalists worked.

There, in a distant corner, I found my old friend and colleague from my Jerusalem days, Petronius Laconicus. He was slumped over his desk wearing a beer-stained toga and an exhausted expression that made him look about 200 years old.

'*Quo vadis*, Laconicus old son?' I greeted him cheerfully.

'Who is that who disturbs my repose?' he muttered, looking up. 'Ah, Ben Bartholomew, second-rate thief-taker turned second-rate lawyer: who are you cheating today?'

'I'm just trying to turn an honest denarius, old friend, that and no more. But why this miserable face and haunted look around the eyes?'

'Our regular chariot-race tipster is on holiday, visiting a sick camel in Cairo or something, so I have been ordered to tip the winners of tomorrow's races for the late edition. What do I know about chariot races?'

'I see the problem.'

'All I know is that the chariot is the one with wheels and the horse is the one with a leg at each corner. And I have to write the tips?!'

'If only the punters knew,' I laughed.

'But if you give me an excuse to put down this miserable pen for a few minutes, then you are welcome, old friend. What can I do for you?'

'Information, please.'

'Just like the old days?'

'Exactly.'

'Are you back on a case? Yes, of course you are. What sort of case?'

'Missing persons.'

'Will there be a story in it for me?'

'I doubt it. A missing teenager. But you'll help anyway, won't you?'

'What do you want to know?'

'Take a look at this list of temples. There are seven listed: I recognise two of them, the rest are unknown to me — there are just so many temples in the city. Do the names mean anything to you?'

Laconicus held the piece of parchment I handed him at arm's length and squinted at it.

'Hmmm…most of these I know. What do you want, addresses?'

'Yes, and any background you can add.'

'Okay. First on the list: The Temple of the Great Clockmaker.'

'That one I have heard of, everybody has. The big temple with the giant gear-wheel on the front…'

'It's a cog-wheel.'

'A what?'

'A giant cog-wheel — like out of a clock.'

'Okay, cog-wheel then. And we all know they have secret handshakes and they give each other jobs and generally look out for each other.'

'That's them,' agreed Laconicus. 'Next is The Temple that Matters. This mob like to think of themselves as the "religion of scientists" but most of their members are technicians, mechanics and amateur inventors rather than true scientists.'

'Then there's The Nothingness Temple.'

'Never heard of that one. I'll make some inquiries for you.'

'What about The Temple of the Golden Eye?'

'Yep, I've heard of them all right. I had to write a feature about them once. Their literature is all long words and long sentences. I could never work out whether it was dense waffle, or whether it was profound and I was dense.'

'What about The One Temple? Does that name mean anything to you?'

'Again — yes. It's one of those religions that comes from the eastern provinces of the far-flung Roman Empire. Inner calmness through contemplating your navel — that sort of thing.'

'Then there's The Inner Temple. I've read about them in your newspaper.'

'I guess everyone has — mostly in the social columns. It's the religion of the rich these days, the current fad, the fashion of the moment. Twelve months from now it'll be last year's religion and no one will want to know.'

'And finally there's The Haunted Temple.'

'That's another one I've not heard of. But again, I'll make some inquiries. Now let me get you addresses for the others.'

A few minutes later I had the addresses of five of the seven pagan temples on Abigail's list jotted down on a scrap of parchment and careful tucked away in the belt of my tunic.

'Now, tell me more about the case, Ben,' said Laconicus, clasping his hands behind his head and leaning back in his chair. His puffy face, the product of years of self-indulgence, took on the sly grin of a hack after a story, as he said, 'perhaps I can help with that too.'

'Well, it's a missing persons case, as I said. Her name is Abigail Jacobson, seventeen years of age, only child of a nice, middle-class Jewish couple, Joe and Hannah Jacobson. She's a quiet, studious sort of girl, not many friends, not given to wild habits so I gather.'

'Not the usual teenage runaway then?'

'Precisely.'

'Last seen?'

'Last seen on Tuesday morning when she left home to visit the city library.'

'Library? Definitely not your typical adolescent!'

I went on to give Laconicus a description of the girl and asked him to spread the word among his contacts that I was looking for her.

'In fact,' I went on, 'you can suggest that if anyone with information comes to me there will be a generous reward in it for them. Joe Jacobson has given me enough leeway to promise that.'

'And the temples? Where do they come in?'

'She's been on a religious kick — visiting a string of pagan temples to, as her father put it, "see what each one has to offer." From the heading on that list of temple names, she appears to have been searching for truth.'

'I could have told her where to find that,' said Laconicus sourly, '— at the bottom of a bottle, that's where. Preferably a bottle of overproof rum — the genuine Egyptian stuff!'

As I made my way back across town through the thickening twilight my head was buzzing with questions.

Was Abigail Jacobson still alive? Was she being held prisoner? Or was she missing by choice? She had taken nothing with her: no clothes, not even her beloved books. Kidnapped? Or killed? But by whom? And why?

So far, the mystery of the disappearance of Abigail Jacobson was all questions and no answers.

I arrived back at our little apartment above the office just as twilight was fading into night.

Rachel was there ahead of me, and the delicious smell of Momma's chicken soup came wafting through from the kitchen.

'Darling,' said Rachel, drawing me to one side and speaking in a whisper, 'when is your mother going back home to Jerusalem?'

'Don't you like having her here, my pet?' I asked.

'I like having *you* here,' she replied, 'and I like having you to myself.'

'I will speak to her.'

'Oh, will you, Ben? Tonight?'

'Yes, tonight. I promise.'

CHAPTER 4

'Now, how did you get on at the library?' I asked.

'For my first assignment as a detective — not too badly,' she replied smugly as she snuggled into my side.

'Well...come on, cough up. What did you learn?'

'I showed the snapshot to a number of the staff and several of them recognised her. One of the older librarians said he had seen Abigail quite often. He said she used to haunt the 100 to 299 section.'

'Which is...?'

'Philosophy and religion.

'Which fits in with what her parents told us. So she really was the studious type, then.'

'Yes. And we can safely assume that her interest in exploring different religious ideas was genuine.'

'Fair enough,' I said. 'Now, what about last Tuesday: was she there on Tuesday morning?'

'Yes. The young girl at the borrowing counter saw her arrive.'

'At what time?'

'I asked that. She wasn't sure, but she thought around the middle of the morning.'

'And she was certain it was Abigail, and certain it was Tuesday?'

'Absolutely.'

'Well, that seems to nail that down. And when did she leave the library?'

'That's where my good fortune ran out. No one actually saw her go, but they were all certain that she was gone by the time lunch was over.'

'So, at the latest, we can say she was gone by…what? Two o'clock?'

'Yes, at least by then. Possibly an hour, or even two hours before then.'

'So she spent between two and four hours at the city library. Does that sound about right?'

'It does. But it doesn't help us much,' said Rachel, snuggling her head into my shoulder.

'It doesn't answer the really big question: where did Abigail go when she walked out of the library? Do you have any suggestions, my love?'

'None, I'm afraid. And I asked the library staff, but they couldn't help. Abi spoke to none of them about her plans for the day, and they had no suggestions as to where she might have been heading when she left.'

'If they're telling us the truth.'

'Now, what did *you* find out, sweetheart?'

I told Rachel about my trip to the newspaper and my conversation with Petronius Laconicus, showed her the list of temple addresses I had collected, and explained my plans for the next day.

Later, when dinner was over, the dishes washed and all three of us were sitting in our tiny front room, Rachel and I on the sofa and Momma in an armchair in the opposite corner knitting, my wife murmured, 'Ben darling, now, how about…' She nudged me with her elbow and pointed towards Momma.

'Ah, yes,'

'Well…?'

'Excuse me, Momma.'

She looked up from her knitting.

'Yes, Benjamin? You have something to say to me?'

'I just…just…just wanted to include you in our conversation — that's all.'

'That's nice, Benjamin. You were talking about your case earlier. I was listening. My heart goes out to that poor girl's mother; she must be suffering.'

'Yes, I think Hannah's taking it pretty hard. The other thing is…'

'Do you think she could be kidnapped?'

'Hannah?'

'The girl. What is her name? Abigail?'

'Yes, Abigail. And, yes…'

'Kidnapped, she could be? At this very moment?'

'Yes, she…'

'You should be out looking for her now, my boy!'

'Look? Where should I look? Abi's parents searched thoroughly before coming to me. And I've put the word out through Laconicus that I'm looking for the girl and will pay for information. I'm hoping that will produce dividends fast.'

'Ben…' hissed Rachel, digging her elbow sharply into my side.

'And there's one other thing, Momma…' I continued.

'If you don't mind, Benjamin my boy, I will ask you to save it for the morning. I am a very tired old Momma and I must go to bed now.'

As she spoke she rose, with some difficulty, from the armchair, spilling her knitting over the floor. I scrabbled around collecting needles and wool, and as I handed them over Momma said, 'Whatever you want to say you can tell me on the way to synagogue in the morning. Goodnight, Benjamin; goodnight, Rachel.'

And with that she waddled up the stairs to the guest bedroom.

Rachel sat on the sofa, her arms folded, a scowl on her face. I looked at her and shrugged my shoulders.

'I tried,' I said.

'Not very hard,' she replied.

'Tomorrow,' I said.

'You'd better,' she said firmly.

'I will! I will! Trust me.'

But the next morning as all three of us walked to synagogue together I didn't raise the issue of her departure with Momma. It didn't feel like the right time or place.

Later, I thought.

White, square, and rather plain on the outside, the synagogue inside was a double-colonnaded meeting hall, filled with wooden benches to seat the congregation. A special alcove facing the main entrance held the ark, or wooden chest, containing the scrolls of the Law and the Prophets: God's words. I sat in the men's seats, and Rachel and Momma in the women's section.

The chief officer called us to worship by reminding us that God is God: 'Keep His commandments carefully in mind,' he intoned. 'Teach them to your children. Talk about them when you are sitting at home, when you are out walking, at bedtime and before breakfast!'

As the service proceeded in the usual manner, with the attendant fetching the scrolls of God's great book from the ark and bringing them in turn to the reading desk, my mind was preoccupied with the disappearance of Abigail Jacobson and I was not paying very close attention until one of the men stood up to read Psalm 19.

'A poem by King David,' he began. 'The heavens are telling the glory of God; they are a marvellous display of His craftsmanship. Day and night they keep on telling about God. Without a sound or word, silent in the skies, their message reaches out to all the world. The sun lives in the heavens where God placed it and moves out across the skies as radiant as a bridegroom going to his wedding, or as joyous as an athlete looking forward to a race! The sun crosses the heavens from end to end and nothing can hide from its heat.'

As I heard these words I closed my eyes and I could picture the sheer beauty and majesty of the universe: the brilliant gold of sunrise; the blazing fire of sunset; the terror of a thunderstorm; and the gentleness of a wheat-field on a spring afternoon; the exquisite beauty of birds and butterflies; the rugged magnificence of snow-capped mountains; and the splendour of the starry sky at night — a world charged with the grandeur of God!

While all this was flashing through my mind the reader was continuing: 'God's laws are perfect. They protect us, make us wise, and give us joy and light. God's laws are pure, eternal, just. They are more desirable than gold. They are sweeter than honey dripping from a honeycomb. They warn us away from harm and give success to those who obey them.'

Once again, on hearing those words, I felt that sense of astonishment charge through me, like a mild electric shock, at the renewed realisation that the God whose grandeur fills the universe has bothered to communicate with mere human beings!

Meanwhile, the reader was still reading from

Psalm 19: 'But how can I ever know what sins are lurking in my heart? Cleanse me from these hidden faults and keep me from deliberate wrongs; help me to stop doing them. Only then can I be free of guilt and innocent of some great crime. May my spoken and unspoken thoughts be pleasing even to you, O Lord, my Rock and my Redeemer.'

Rachel and I knew that God had intervened in human history in an ultimate and decisive way through Jesus Christ — his own Son. We were followers of Jesus, the one promised in God's great book of the law and the prophets: God's King, God's appointed ruler of planet earth. Jesus' role as the giver of life, as the only one with the real authority to rule every life, is established by his resurrection. As I had discovered in an earlier investigation. But, to the best of our knowledge, we were the only Christians in Caesarea so we still came to the synagogue each week.

Where else, we asked ourselves, could we worship the maker of the universe who, astonishingly, chooses to dirty his hands by cleaning up the mess of human lives?

CHAPTER 5

After the service we all stood around outside in the courtyard chatting, as we did every week.

Joe and Hannah Jacobson were there, I noticed, surrounded by a group of their close friends comforting them in their anxiety. But there was one man in particular I was looking for, and when I spotted him on the opposite side of the courtyard I beckoned Rachel and we walked across.

'Good morning, Cornelius,' I said.

'Morning, Ben,' he replied. 'Morning, Rachel.'

Publius Cornelius was a Captain in the Roman army stationed in Caesarea. He had taken to coming to synagogue whenever he wasn't on duty, and sitting in the screened gallery for non-Jews at the back. Not being a Jew by birth, he belonged to a category known as 'God-fearers.' A good man, his genial face had the tanned, weather-beaten appearance that recorded his life in the military service of his emperor — mostly served out of doors in all kinds of weather.

Of Italian origin, his hair was probably once black, but now it was steel grey, and clipped very short, in the Roman manner. In fact, it was trimmed so short that it stood straight up on top of his head, giving him a perpetually surprised expression. But in the months I had known him, I had learned that the expression was misleading. Having a sharp mind and astute judgement, Cornelius was rarely caught by surprise.

'Have you heard about the disappearance of Abigail Jacobson?' I asked.

'Indeed I have,' replied the captain. 'I heard on the day that Joe came to headquarters to report her disappearance.'

'Well, Joe has asked me to take charge of the search,' I explained, 'and I was wondering if you could help.'

'I've already urged the city watch to ask questions and keep their eyes open. I don't think there's much more I can do.'

'Oh, but there is,' I said. 'Something criminal has happened, Cornelius, foul play is involved.'

'Are you sure?' he asked.

'Absolutely. The first thing I've done is to check on Abigail's character. On the evidence of her parents, of what we found in her room, and of her behaviour on the day she disappeared, I don't think she planned to leave. And that almost certainly means that she did not leave willingly.'

'Yes…I see.'

'My best guess is that she has been kidnapped or,' I looked around to make sure that Joe and Hannah could not hear, 'murdered.'

'But why?', asked the captain. Decency and integrity were second nature to Cornelius, and that made it hard for him to understand what motivated other types of human beings. He had risen in the ranks of the Roman army, without the benefit of a noble patron, simply on the basis of his own capacity, loyalty and reliability. 'I can think of no reason,' he continued, 'for killing an innocent, harmless girl like Abigail. Can you?'

'Not so far, but I'm checking.'

'And as for kidnapping...well...there's been no ransom demand, has there?'

'That's true,' I replied.

'So, then — surely if she had been taken, there would have been a demand for money by now?'

'It would depend on *why* she was taken.'

'You know the underworld better than I do, Ben, why would kidnappers not demand money?'

'Perhaps they intended to and something went wrong with their plans. Or perhaps they didn't want money from Abi's parents, but from someone else.'

'Such as?'

'Well, there are certain foreign princes who will pay handsomely to add a pretty, dark-haired teenager to their harem.'

'White-slavers, you mean?'

'It's a possibility,' I admitted.

Cornelius' weather-beaten face set in a grim mask. 'What can I do to help?' he asked.

'Have there been other, similar disappearances in Caesarea?'

'I don't know. But there could be cases that I haven't heard about. I'm only a captain, you know.'

'Could you find out?'

'Yes, yes, I could. I'll go and talk to the Collator at headquarters first thing tomorrow.'

'Great. And let me know as soon as you find out something.'

'I'll do that. Anything else?'

'Hold a watching brief for me. I have a feeling this case is going to break wide open pretty soon. I'd like to hear as soon as headquarters knows. Can you be my eyes and ears, Cornelius?'

'I can, and I will,' said the soldier briskly, almost

clicking his heels together with a snap as he said the words.

'Providing,' he continued, 'you keep me in touch, step by step, with your investigation. Will you do that for me?'

'It's a promise.'

All through my conversation Rachel had been standing silently by my side, looking very serious and very subdued.

'Ben,' she said, as Cornelius walked away, 'you think she's dead, don't you?'

I nodded my head slowly.

'I have a gut feeling about this one, Rachel,' I said quietly. 'And my gut is telling me that Abigail has been murdered.'

There was a sharp intake of breath from Rachel when I said the word 'murdered' and her eyes moistened.

Our dark mood was invaded by Momma, who waddled over chatting happily.

'You know the best part about synagogue, Benjamin my boy?'

Before I could answer, Momma ploughed on at the top of her voice.

'...It's the recipes you get afterwards. Mrs Solomons — you know Mrs Solomons, don't you? Ah, yes, of course you do, her son Sam is in this same dreadful private eye business.'

'I knew him in Jerusalem,' I started to say, but before I could get the words out Momma was saying: 'You knew him in Jerusalem, I know you did, don't tell me you didn't.'

Momma paused to catch her breath and then hurtled onwards, 'Well, Mrs Solomons, she gave me a new recipe for matzo balls and I gave her my recipe for gefillte fish in return. And then she told me what Mrs Levi told her about what Mr Danielson has been up to. Mrs Danielson doesn't know, of course — the wife is always the last to know....'

And so it went on. And on. And on. And on.

I sort of tuned out, and began taking an interest in the groups of people standing around us in the court-yard in front of the synagogue. Rachel has better manners than me: she listened politely to what Momma had to say, nodding her head occasionally in agreement.

A vigorous and energetic voice drew my attention to a conversation that was going on behind my back.

'That's right!' the voice was saying, 'Jesus, the carpenter's son from Nazareth, he is the one, the anointed one, the one the Law and the Prophets speak of.'

There was some murmured response, and then the rapid, somewhat high-pitched voice continued: 'Why don't you come to lunch at my place today? My wife Helen won't mind — at least, I'm pretty sure she won't mind. And I can tell you about the things that Jesus taught and did.'

This interested me, so I turned around to take a look at the speaker. He turned out to be a tall, slim young man with unruly hair and an animated face. The audience he was haranguing consisted of Laban and Martha Ephraim, a newly married couple who had only recently joined the congregation, having moved to Caesarea from the town of Lydda.

Eventually they accepted the invitation to lunch, and addresses were exchanged.

'Excuse me,' I said, as Laban and Martha left, 'I couldn't help overhearing what you were saying just now — and I wanted to tell you that my wife Rachel and I are followers of this Jesus of whom you speak.'

'Dear brother!' cried the tall young man, giving me a huge smile. 'It is wonderful to find other believers already here in the city. My name is Philip, by the way. I'm from Jerusalem.'

'You've come from there recently?'

'Indirectly, but recently.'

'Indirectly?'

'From Jerusalem via Samaria, the Gaza Road, Azotus and Joppa.'

'You took the long way, then?'

'After a fashion. And you are...?'

'I'm Ben Bartholomew, and this is my wife Rachel,' I said, dragging Rachel away from Momma's monologue for a moment. 'Rachel, meet Philip.'

'How do you do, Philip.'

'Your husband tells me that you two are followers of Jesus. Is this so?'

'Yes, it is,' said Rachel defiantly, chin held high, this being a subject on which we have been put rather on the defensive by other members of the congregation.

'Wonderful! I am delighted to meet you, dear sister,' enthused Philip. 'I'm trying to organise a weekly meeting for followers of Jesus in this city and those who choose to join us. Are you interested?'

'Why, certainly,' she said with a warm smile, 'we're interested, aren't we, Ben?'

I agreed that we were and Philip promised to make contact with us in the course of the next few days.

Momma, Rachel and I walked home from synagogue in silence — Momma being talked out (at last!) and Rachel and I having much to think about.

It was much later, well after the sun had set and the darkness outside had become total, that the three of us were sitting around in our front room when we were disturbed by a noise.

I heard it — a dull thud — but I intended to ignore it until Rachel spoke.

'Did you hear that, Ben?'

'I heard something.'

'It was someone knocking on our front door. You'd better go and check.'

'No, it wasn't! It didn't sound at all like a door-knock.'

'It did to me, and if you won't check, I will!'

'All right! All right! Don't get your toga in a twist. I'll go down and check.'

I made my way down two flights of stairs to our street door. This I unbolted, swung open, and looked out. There was no one on the doorstep, and no one in sight.

I stepped out onto the front porch and looked up and down the darkened street. No one.

Then I turned to re-enter the house, and that's when I saw it: a heavy, bronze knife, of Roman manufacture I would guess, its blade buried deep in the timber of my front door, the handle still trembling.

Pinned to the door by the dagger was a scrap of parchment. On that parchment were scrawled two words: 'Forget Abigail.'

A cold shiver ran down my spine, and I decided I would feel much safer indoors.

Using the edge of my robe, so as not to spoil any finger-prints, I eased the dagger out of the door, took the note by one corner, and carried both upstairs — carefully locking and bolting the door behind me.

'What was it?' asked Rachel.

'A message,' I replied.

Startled by the grim tone in my voice she looked up.

'Read it,' I said, holding up the note by one corner. 'Don't touch it, in case there are finger-prints — just read it.'

' "Forget Abigail" Where did you find it?'

'It was pinned to our front door by this nasty little weapon,' I explained, holding up the dagger. 'We are being warned off, Rachel my love, we are being firmly warned off.'

CHAPTER 6

'A warning? What sort of warning?' cried Momma, dropping her knitting.

'Nothing for you to worry about, Momma,' I replied.

'You stand there holding a giant sword that could kill an army and you tell me not to worry? What sort of a mother do you think I am?'

'It's not a giant sword, Momma, it's just a little dagger. Well...not so little, maybe. But it's just a dagger.'

'It's a dagger with a message already,' said Momma.

'That's true,' I admitted.

'It's a threat,' said Rachel, examining the elaborately carved snake on the hilt of the dagger, 'warning us away from the Abigail Jacobson case.'

'Then you should get away from it.' cried Momma. 'I don't want that my Benjamin should get hurt. Or my Rachel either, for that matter.'

'Momma,' I said firmly, 'I am not going to retreat from this case.'

'I want you should beat a retreat! I want you should beat it to death! Get out of this case, Benjamin, it is far too dangerous!'

'Now you stay calm, Momma. People often make threats they don't mean. Especially vague threats like this one.'

'That is not a vague dagger, Benjamin. Bronze it is, vague it ain't. We could all be at risk: you, Rachel, even me maybe.'

I seized my opportunity and plunged in: 'I don't want you in danger, Momma, so why don't you go home to Jerusalem? See how Poppa has been getting on without you.'

'If you think I will run away from danger, Benjamin my boy, you are backing entirely the wrong chariot. I am staying right here, beside you and Rachel.'

Rachel and I exchanged a look, but we said nothing. Later, when Momma had gone up to bed I said, 'Well, I tried, but she refused to leave.'

'I don't know that your timing was very good,' said Rachel with a curl of her lip. 'You should try again another time.'

'I will, I will, I promise you.'

'And just how seriously do you take this threat?'

'I think we should both be careful from now on. I'm not giving up the case, but I'm not going to take any foolish risks either. In fact, it would be best if you leave this case to me from now on...'

'Oh no you don't!' she interrupted. 'Before you are many kalends older, Ben my love, you will discover that I do not give up detecting just because there is a hint of danger.'

Looking at the firm and determined expression on her face I knew that she meant what she said, and I admitted defeat: 'Okay then,' I said, 'we will face the threat and tackle the task together. Gird up your loins then...'

'You leave my loins out of this!' said Rachel with a giggle, as she threw her arms around me and hugged me close.

'Gird up your loins, as I was saying in a most poetic fashion, and tomorrow we will begin investigating Abigail's list of temples.'

The next morning, as soon as the breakfast things had been cleared away, Rachel and I left the house together, telling Momma to lock the door behind us and admit no one during our absence.

The first temple on the list was The Temple of the Great Clockmaker, which was located on a broad thoroughfare leading down to the Forum.

It was a large, square red-brick building, with fake marble pillars giving the whole thing a slightly Greek appearance. Set into the front wall were tall, double doors of polished bronze. Climbing the front steps I tried these and found them unlocked. They swung silently inwards on well-oiled hinges, and Rachel and I walked into the dim and shadowy interior of the temple.

When my eyes had adjusted to the pale light that filtered in through a single sky-light high in the vaulted ceiling above our heads, I noticed the two giant cog-wheels. One was set vertically into the wall while the other was set horizontally into the floor beneath it. These wheels turned constantly, slowly and silently, their cogs meshing as they turned.

High up on one of the side walls was a slogan painted in large, golden letters: 'Whatever is, is right.' On the opposite wall was another slogan which read: 'Reason is the candle that lights the world.'

When I looked down from the slogans I discovered that three cowled figures, wearing the dark-brown habits of monks, were advancing towards us from a distant corner of the meeting hall.

'Cop these three,' hissed Rachel in a sharp whisper. 'Are these the three stupid monkeys, or what?'

'The expression is "wise monkeys," ' I corrected.

'You stick to your expression, I'll stick to mine,' she responded.

As the three robed and hooded figures drew close, the middle one spoke: 'Good morning, can I help?'

'Good morning,' I said, 'I'm Ben Bartholomew, this is my wife Rachel.'

'Greetings and salutations. I am called Brother Advocatus…'

'I didn't know advocatus were in season at the moment,' murmured Rachel in my ear.

'…this is Brother Auxilium,' he said, gesturing to his left, and then, turning to his right, added, 'and this is his twin, Brother Ibid. How may we help you?'

'May I speak to someone in charge, please?'

'What is the nature of your inquiry?'

'A teenage girl — Abigail Jacobson — has disappeared, and I've been employed by her parents to investigate.'

'Have you any reason for assuming that she has visited us here at the temple?'

'I know she has,' I replied, expressing a certainty I did not feel. 'Do you remember the name?'

'Abigail, you said?'

'That's right: Abigail Jacobson.'

'No…I can't say that I do.'

Rachel pulled out the snapshot of Abigail that Joe had given us. 'Take a look at this,' she said. 'Do you recognise her?'

'Hmmm…I'm afraid not.'

His companions did not speak but silently shook their heads.

'But someone else might,' I persisted, 'so may I speak to someone in charge?'

'Yes. Yes, I think it would be best.' So saying, he

turned on his heels and led the way across the polished timber floor to a small door in the far wall. Rachel and I followed him with the other two cowled figures close behind us. As we walked, Rachel glanced at me, and without a word being spoken I could tell what she was thinking: if this was a trap we were now hemmed in and would find escape difficult.

On the other side of the low doorway was a dimly lit corridor. Brother Advocatus led us down this, around a corner, and through a second door.

Upon entering, we found ourselves in a kind of library: the walls were panelled in dark timber, there were book-shelves on three sides filled with leather-bound volumes, while the sparse furniture (a plain table and several straight-backed chairs) were made from the same dark timber as the panelling.

'Wait here,' ordered Brother Advocatus abruptly, closing the door behind him as he left.

'Well…' said Rachel, 'what do you make of…'

She didn't finish her sentence, but just let her glance run around the room.

'I don't know,' I said. For reasons that we could not have explained, we were both speaking in hushed tones. 'Let's wait and see.'

We didn't have to wait long.

After only a few minutes the door was flung open and a tall, aristocratic figure entered.

'Morning,' he said briskly, 'I'm Brother Argumentum, the Supervising Mechanic of this temple. I believe you are looking for some missing girl.'

'It's Bacon, isn't it!' I said with a sudden gasp of recognition. 'Alexander Bacon!'

'Ah…yes…yes, that is the name by which I am

known in the world beyond the temple, but here I am Brother Argumentum.'

'Sorry,' I murmured, 'yes, of course. Brother Argumentum, we are investigating the disappearance of Abigail Jacobson.'

'On whose authority?'

'On behalf of her parents.'

'I see. Please continue.'

'And we have reason to believe she was a visitor to this temple. Do you know the name? Do you recognise this picture?'

As I spoke, Rachel produced the snapshot.

'Yes,' he said slowly. But he took so long to answer that I had a chance to look him over. Far from wearing the monkish habit of his underlings he was dressed like a courtier from the Governor's palace: all velvet and silk, in robes that made him look like a dandy.

'Yes, I believe she did visit us. I had a conversation with her once. She wanted to know what we believed, and why.'

'And what did you say to her?'

'Exactly what I would say to any inquirer: that our starting point is Human Reason. It is Reason that is the Inner Light, the Candle of God. Reason, and Reason alone, is sufficient to tell us all we need to know about the world.'

'And what does it tell you? What is your view of the world?'

'In summary, there are just six key points. First, that God is the Great Clockmaker, the eternal first cause, the maker and "winder-up" of the universe. Second, that the universe runs according to the blueprint — it is a pre-determined, closed system — each part turning mechanically in its place. Third, that human beings are just part of the clockwork, part of what we call "the movement." Fourth, that human reason can, by observation, tell us all there is to know about the machinery of the universe. Fifth, that the machine is functioning normally: whatever is, is right, and there are no other moral judgements to be made. And sixth, that human history is merely the ticking of the minutes and the chiming of the hours.'

'Not exactly a warm and wonderful picture of the universe,' I commented.

'That's the way it is,' he responded tartly. 'Just use your reason and you'll see.'

'And was Abigail satisfied?' asked Rachel. 'Did she find what you told her helpful?'

'Possibly not, since she never came back again.'

'So when was the last time you saw her?' I asked.

He thought for a moment, and then replied, 'Possibly six weeks ago.'

Chapter 7

'Do you believe him?' asked Rachel, when we were back in the dusty street, surrounded by rumbling farm carts and impatient chariot-drivers.

'I think I do,' I replied thoughtfully, as I dodged a bellowing charioteer and his galloping horse.

'Why?'

'Well, think about the heading at the top of Abi's list of temples. She was searching for truth, remember? And I doubt that she would have found much truth in their philosophy.'

'Yes, I guess you're right.'

'The more I think about it, the more certain I become that she would have lost interest in that lot pretty quickly. Once you see the world in clockwork terms — just ticking over endlessly and steadily — then you lose the distinction between right and wrong. If this world is just a piece of machinery, then their slogan is quite correct: "Whatever is, is right." If people suffer, then that must be right because it is part of the machinery of the world. If people see no hope and no purpose in life, then that must be right too — it's just the way the machine runs.'

'And Abi was a bright girl, so she would have picked that up.'

'Yes, indeed.'

'Ben! Do you realise what I just did?'

'What was that?'

'I just said that Abi "was" not "is." I spoke as if she is dead!' said Rachel. 'I feel just awful about doing that.'

'I understand. Don't be too hard on yourself.'

We walked some way in silence, and then I said, 'There's something else about the philosophy of that temple that, I believe, would have driven Abi away.'

'What's that?'

'The fact that they would regard human personality as just another "fact" of the universe — just another little cog-wheel. How could truth be found in such a low view of human significance?'

'I see the point. By the way, Ben, who is that "Brother Argumentum" really? You recognised him, didn't you?'

'He's a lawyer — a fairly stuffy old-fashioned lawyer who specialises in company tax law. When he's not at the temple playing at being a bigwig he's the senior partner in Bacon, Appolonius & Bacon.'

'Why would he be interested in the temple?'

'Like the law firm, I think it's one of those "father-to-son" things. His father was a Clockmaker before him, so when he came of age he donned the symbolic apron of the watchmaker, went through the initiation ceremony, took the oaths of secrecy, and became a Clockmaker himself.'

When we got home Momma had taken a message for me: I was to ring Laconicus as soon as possible. I grabbed the telephone and dialled his number: IV-II-VII-IV-I-IX-IX.

'Laconicus? It's Bartholomew here, what's the news?'

'A couple of things, Ben. First, I've identified another of those temples on the list. Remember there were two of them that I didn't recognise?'

'Yeah, I remember: The Nothingness Temple and The Haunted Temple.'

'That's right. Well, I've made some inquiries and I've tracked down The Nothingness Temple. It's a basement place in the docks area of the city. The full name is The Nothingness Temple and Coffee Bar.'

When I had scribbled down the address I asked, 'What about The Haunted Temple?'

'Nothing on that so far but I'm still checking.'

'Thanks for that.'

'Right. I also wanted to let you know that I've spread the word around about you looking for the girl, and about the possibility of a reward. With any luck you'll get a response before too long.'

'I've already had a response.'

'A lead?'

'A threat!' I said, and told him about the note pinned to the door with a dagger.

'What do you make of it?' he asked.

'I reckon that somebody is very nervous.'

'Hmmm, and nervous people are people with secrets to hide. Perhaps there is a story in this for me after all.'

'I'll keep you in touch,' I said as I rang off.

No sooner had I put down the phone than it began to jangle noisily. I picked it up and heard Joe Jacobson's voice.

'Ben, I know you'd contact us if you had anything to report, but Hannah and I are so worried I just had to ring. Have you made any progress?'

'We've eliminated some possibilities,' I said, choosing my words carefully, 'and there's been one tentative contact from a party who may know the truth about Abigail's fate.' (I was thinking, of course, about the anonymous threat.)

'That's all?' He sounded disappointed.

'So far, but we're working on it. While you're on the phone you can tell me something.'

'Anything.'

'Which college is Abigail enrolled in?'

'Oh, Abigail is not a college student!'

'But…but…I had the impression that Abigail was engaged in full-time studies.'

'No, not at all. She's a studious type of girl, but she's not going to college. She works at the Governor's palace. She's a typist in the civil service.'

'Then how come she wasn't at work last Tuesday?'

'Because she's on her annual leave. She's been working at the palace for exactly twelve months, so now she has two weeks' leave.'

'Oh, I see,' I said lamely, silently cursing clients who don't tell all the facts, and myself for making assumptions.

'You'd better give me the name of her employer at the palace. Her disappearance might have something to do with her work.'

'No, it hasn't.'

'How do you know?'

'I asked them last week — as soon as Abi disappeared I went and spoke to them.'

'You'd still better give me a name, and I'll pay the palace a visit — there might be something you missed.'

'Very well, if you like. Abigail works as a typist and receptionist for a very senior public servant — a man named Mediocritas.'

'Okay, I'll check him out. Is this the only job she's had since she left school?'

'Oh no. Abi had two other jobs before she started

at the palace. She didn't stay long at either, though — she didn't like them.'

'You'd better give me the names of her previous employers — I'll check them out as well.'

'If you think it's really necessary.'

'I do.'

'Very well. Abi worked as a typist, firstly at De Mortuis, the undertakers. Dreadful place, always smelled of embalming fluid. She left there after only a month and went to work for a firm of tax accountants: their name is Cursus & Minimis. But she found the work boring, and stayed only six weeks. Then a year ago she got this very good job at the palace.'

'I've made a note,' I said. 'I'll investigate all those places. And I'll keep you in touch, Joe, don't you worry.'

He rang off just as Rachel was walking into the room with a fresh cup of coffee. I told her about Abigail's employment. She was as surprised as I was.

'Somehow I got the impression she was a student.'

' "Studious" but not a "student," ' I said. 'There is a difference.'

Just then the phone rang again. It was Cornelius.

He was calling to hold me to my promise to report on the investigation to him, step by step. I gave him a detailed report on our visit to the first temple on Abigail's list.

'What do you make of it, Ben?' he asked when I finished. 'How much truth is there in the Clockmaker view of the world?'

'Precious little,' I replied. 'It strikes me as being far too convenient.'

'But they do believe in God, don't they?'

'It depends what you mean by "believe" and by "God." They give assent to an idea of their own invention. But there is no sense of commitment to the God who is there. God is not some second cousin from Cairo! God can't be made "safe"! And, surely, that's what they aim to do. What they want is a "God" who demands no obedience and never intervenes in the world. That does not have the ring of truth about it. It has the smell of fear about it: the aroma of agnosticism, the fear that if they ever really made contact with God he would make demands on their lives.'

'By the way, Ben,' said Cornelius, 'you asked me to check on whether there had been any other disappearances, similar to Abigail's, in the last few weeks in Caesarea.'

'Yeah, what did you find?'

'Nothing, I'm afraid, not a sausage. According to the city watch there have been the usual disappearances (sailors jumping ship, drunken camel-drivers, and so on) but no other teenage girls.'

'I see,' I said thoughtfully as I sipped my coffee. 'So whatever has happened to Abigail, it looks like a one-off.'

'Sorry...that doesn't help you much, Ben.'

'It eliminates one possibility, and that's useful. Thank you, Cornelius.'

'Call me if there's anything else I can do,' he said as he rang off.

'You heard that?' I asked, turning to Rachel.

'Yes, I did. So what next?'

'Back to Abigail's list. Which temple is next?'

'Ah, let me see now. The Temple that Matters — a very modest name!'

'Well, *tempus fugit* — let's get a move on.'

We found The Temple that Matters in an industrial suburb on the southern edge of the city. It was a rather plain and functional lecture hall. The exterior walls had been cement-rendered and painted white. But that had been some years ago; the blistering Mediterranean sun was peeling the paint, and another coat was definitely called for.

Standing immediately behind the neglected lecture hall, on the same block of land, was what looked like a luxury hotel. Did this have any connection with the temple? I wondered.

Inside the temple was quiet and cool. There were stackable chairs arranged in rows facing a plain wooden lectern, on the wall above which, in bold black and white lettering, was a text that read: 'Matter is all that is, or was, or ever will be. Mind is brain, personality is chemistry.'

'Odd sort of temple,' remarked Rachel, 'What sort of worship goes on here?'

'That's what we're here to find out,' I muttered.

Set into the wall were three glass cases. We walked over to take a closer look at them.

The first one contained a microscope, with a small brass plate stating: 'What I cannot see does not exist.'

The next held a test-tube, and here the brass plate read: 'What I cannot hold does not exist.'

'What's this?' asked Rachel, standing in front of the third glass case. 'A set of scales?'

I walked over and joined her.

'No,' I said, 'it's a balance — a laboratory balance.'

This time the little brass plate carried the caption: 'What I cannot measure does not exist.'

'Peculiar, if you ask me,' said Rachel.

I was about to add my own comment when a voice behind us said loudly and sharply, 'Can we help you?'

CHAPTER 8

We turned around to find ourselves facing two middle-aged men wearing grey dust-coats.

'Hi!' I said, turning on my warmest smile. 'I'm Ben Bartholomew and this is my wife Rachel.'

'How do you do. I am Brother Proteus,' said one of the two, in a rather flat and gravelly voice. 'And my friend here is Brother Pyrrhus. What can we do for you?'

'We're looking for a girl,' I explained.

'A young woman, really,' added Rachel.

'Huh! You won't find many young women here! That's for sure,' said Brother Proteus.

'Too right! All too true!' said Brother Pyrrhus.

'Her name is Abigail Jacobson, she's seventeen years of age, and she's missing. We know that she visited this temple recently.'

'Did she now? Well, maybe you'd better speak to the boss about that.'

'And who might he be?'

'Brother Nestor — he's in charge around here.'

'May we speak to him then?' asked Rachel with her sweetest smile.

The two looked at each other for a moment, and then one of them said, 'We'll fetch him,' and they slouched off together at a foot-dragging pace.

'What a strange pair!' whispered Rachel, 'What are they? Janitors or something?'

'Personally I'd bet on the something,' I said as I flicked the dust off one of the stackable chairs and sat down, while Rachel paced the empty hall.

Brother Nestor bustled in through a door at the rear of the hall, a small, middle-aged man with a bald dome of a head, a fringe of rusty-brown hair and a tiny toothbrush moustache on his upper lip. He was wearing dark blue pin-striped trousers, badly in need of pressing and held up by red braces. Under the elastic of the braces was a white business shirt, tie-less, sleeves rolled up, and unbuttoned at the neck. On the end of his nose was a pair of wire-framed spectacles with small, round lenses.

I rose to my feet as we introduced ourselves.

'Please call me Bert — Bert Polly is the name. "Brother Nestor" is my title as secretary of the temple.'

'Well, Mr Polly, I take it you've been told the purpose of our call?'

'I was told only that we had visitors. Those two,' he looked over his shoulder towards the rear of the hall, 'are not very helpful, I'm afraid.'

'We are looking for a missing teenage girl,' explained Rachel briskly, 'named Abigail Jacobson. She visited this temple quite recently.'

Bert Polly looked puzzled for a moment, and then he smiled, 'Ah, yes! Of course! I remember Abigail. A most intelligent young lady.'

'She was here, then?'

'Certainly she was. About five weeks ago.'

'When was the last time you saw her?'

'About five weeks ago. May I suggest that we continue our conversation in more comfortable surroundings?'

'Yes, of course.'

'Follow me, please.'

Rachel and I followed him across the echoing vastness of the lecture hall. A door led into a corridor that connected with the luxury hotel I had noticed behind the temple.

A short walk down a wide hallway over soft, thick-pile carpet brought us to a luxurious lounge-room.

'This is the Senior Common Room,' said Mr Polly, 'we can talk here.'

Rachel and I looked around: the padded leather lounges, the antique tables and book-cases — all of this had cost a pretty denarius. One whole wall was tinted glass, and opened onto an enclosed courtyard in which a marble fountain splashed a gentle trickle of water into a decorative pool.

'Please be seated,' said Bert Polly. 'We might as well be comfortable.'

'And this is very comfortable indeed,' remarked Rachel, under her breath.

'Now, what did you want to ask about that young woman?'

'Well, just how often did Abigail come here?' I inquired.

'Just the once. She spent most of an afternoon here. Attended one of our lectures and then stayed afterwards, asking a great many questions. Very intelligent questions they were too.'

'What was she asking about?'

'Well, what we believe, what we teach, that sort of thing.'

'And what were you able to tell her?'

'I gave her the usual summary of our position. Would you care to hear it?'

'Yes, please.'

'It's a six-point summary. First, matter exists eternally and is all there is. Second, everything can (in principle) be explained in terms of cause and effect — the universe is a closed system. Third, human beings are just biological organisms — just complex collections of chemicals. Fourth, death is extinction. Fifth, history (both natural history and human history) is a sequence of events with no goal and no purpose. And sixth, morality is a convention of human culture.'

'That's it?' asked Rachel, her eyebrows raised.

'That's it. Neat, isn't it?'

'What sort of rituals, or worship, or whatever, do you have here in the temple?' she persisted.

'We have replaced all that mumbo-jumbo with popular lectures on scientific subjects. For instance, we have lectures on the plain person's guide to chemistry, physics, astronomy, biology, geology...and so on.'

'And that's what you told Rachel?'

'Most certainly.'

'How did she respond?'

'As I recall, very quietly. She went away in the end not saying much.'

Rachel and I looked at each other. Without a word we agreed that Abigail had failed to find the truth she was looking for here. Bert Polly took our silence as a cue for him to continue.

'Looked at properly it's a very poetic and romantic story. It begins in the timeless aeons — POW! The Big Bang. All the laws of physics and chemistry go into top gear. The solar system spins into existence. The Earth throbs volcanically. In the primeval soup one-celled amoebae develop, and the great story of life begins. Millions of years from now, our sun will fade out, the whole universe will cool down and darken, and the timeless aeons will once again belong to the dark vacuum. The whole story of humanity is a brief episode between two oblivions. Isn't that just the most wonderful story?'

Mr Polly's face was shining as he blinked at us through his spectacles.

'Ah, thank you for that, Bert' I said. 'May I ask one other thing? It's not connected with Abigail, but it has me puzzled.'

'Ask whatever you wish,' said Polly, smiling comfortably, his arms folded across his plump little stomach.

'All this comfort and luxury — is this part of The Temple that Matters?'

'Not originally. At first there was just the building out front. But over the years, as members have died and left us bequests, we have added this luxury wing and kept the original building as it was, for historical reasons. Or, perhaps, sentimental reasons.'

'But isn't it a rather indulgent use of money?' asked Rachel. 'Couldn't you have found something better to do with it?'

'What? Like helping the poor, or something?'

'Something like that,' said Rachel.

'My dear young woman,' said Mr Polly, rather smugly, 'if matter is all that matters, then the purpose of life is to accumulate as much of it as possible. Surely you can see that?'

'Well, I suppose that I...'

'Of course! Just a moment's thought will convince you that the aim of daily life is comfort. We are true materialists here at The Temple that Matters — in practise as well as in theory.'

Rachel and I thanked Mr Polly for his time, and beat a hasty retreat.

Back outside in the healthy heat of the blazing Mediterranean sun we both felt much better.

'Not much in the way of truth or hope for poor Abigail in that temple,' said Rachel.

'I agree. But many people would not. Many people would find a philosophy endorsing greed and self-indulgence very comfortable indeed.'

'But everyone *dies*!' said Rachel insistently. 'How can any of that stuff make sense, when everyone is headed for the same long-term goal — the grave!'

'Be serious, sweetheart,' I said. 'What do you think people are more interested in: truth or money?'

'Hhhmm...I take your point,' she agreed.

'You know what gets me?'

'What?'

'If the human mind is just a bunch of chemical reactions, how can they be so certain they can *know* anything? Materialists believe everything is explained in terms of cause and effect. That means our minds never *know* anything — they are just caused to think certain things. And that eliminates the whole concept of knowledge.'

'Although from Abi's point of view,' said Rachel, 'even more importantly, they have eliminated hope. There can be no meaning or hope for human beings, since human personality is just a kind of accident.'

'Not what I'd call a fun philosophy,' I remarked.

'So where to next?' asked Rachel.

'Where Abi went next: whichever temple is next on her list. But that's for tomorrow.'

As we made our way back into the centre of Caesarea we passed a construction gang working on yet another aqueduct. Watching the workers clamber back and forth over the wooden scaffolding, it struck me once again that the Romans have an obsession with aqueducts. Or, perhaps, an obsession with water.

A few paces further on we passed one of Caesarea's many public baths, its tiled portico hung with towels drying in the sun, and from inside the sound of water splashing. Yes, that's what it was: an obsession with water.

The street we were on was crowded, as were all the streets in this bustling city. Around us were carts and wagons, and the occasional camel or donkey. All this traffic raised a constant cloud. The dust swirled around our legs, where it stuck to trickles of sweat; around our bodies, where it caught in the folds of our robes; and around our heads, causing us to cover our mouths and blink our eyes.

And as I inhaled a lungful of dust I could suddenly understand the Roman obsession with water. Oh for a deep, cold bath right now!

Our tiny apartment had no room for a proper, splash-all-over bath. All we had was a jug and a basin and a well down the end of the street. Still, I did the best I could with these primitive implements to divest myself of the dust of the day.

Having done so, I called Cornelius, to keep my promise of regular reporting.

I told him in detail about our visit to The Temple that Matters.

'Very interesting, Ben,' was his comment. 'Now give me your evaluation of it.'

'Well, I would think that it represents the dominant world view. It's the way many people think the world is.'

'Well, if it's so popular, what could possibly be wrong with it?'

'Two things. First, does materialism give us adequate reasons for thinking of human beings as valuable? Unique, maybe. But so are gorillas. Could human beings — thrown up by chance by unconscious matter — be worthy and valuable?'

'And second?'

'If my mind is just my brain, an organic thinking machine, how can I trust my thoughts? How can I ever know, for certain, that anything is true?'

'So why does materialism remain so popular?'

'Because at the material level it *does* succeed in explaining a lot about this world. But mainly because many people are just not interested in thinking about it critically at all. It suits them. So why ask questions about it?'

'But Ben,' said Cornelius, 'I *want* to ask questions about it!'

'Then you are wise,' I replied. 'Socrates said that the unexamined life is not worth living. The trouble is, there are too many people who want to pursue comfort, rather than truth.'

CHAPTER 9

Early in the morning, with the first grey light of dawn
in the sky, I was woken by a ringing telephone. I had
to stumble downstairs to the office, since we could
not afford a second extension in the apartment.

'Hello?' I croaked in a voice filled with sleep.

'Ben?'

I acknowledged that I was Ben, I was awake
enough for that.

'It's me, Cornelius. I'm on the early shift at the
palace. A report has just hit my desk from the city
watch. Abigail Jacobson's body has been discovered.'

'Where? When?'

'Overnight. Lying in a ditch beside the Mount
Carmel road — just north of the city. And Ben —
she's been murdered.'

I was stunned into a long silence.

'Ben? Are you still there?' boomed Cornelius'
voice down the phone line.

'Yes…yes, I'm here. I'm thinking.'

'Do you want to come out and see the spot where
she was found before they move the body?'

'Yes, I think I better had.'

'Then meet me at the palace in fifteen minutes and
I'll take you there.'

'Fifteen minutes? I'll be there.'

I hung up the phone and hurried back upstairs. I

crept into the bedroom as quietly as possible, but Rachel was already awake.

'Who was that on the phone?' she asked sleepily.

'You go back to sleep, sweetheart, I'll deal with it.'

'Deal with what?' Now she was sounding rather more awake. 'What needs dealing with?'

'Just leave it to me, Rachel. You get back to sleep.'

That was enough to make her sit up in bed.

'Ben, what's going on?'

Instead of replying I started pulling on a clean toga, and buckling on a pair of sandals.

'Are you paying attention to me? Or are my words going in one orifice and out another? Ben?'

'Yes, I'm listening, dear. But this is a job for me, not you.'

'At least tell me the news!'

'Abigail's body has been found. I'm sorry, Rachel, she's been…murdered.'

'Oh, Ben! That's terrible!'

'Someone's going to have to break the news to Joe and Hannah, and I think it might have to be us.'

'What are you getting dressed for now? It's only just dawn.'

'I'm going out to see the body before they move it.'

'Then I'm coming with you.'

And with that she leaped out of bed, and started to pull on a robe, cloak and sandals.

'You are not coming with me!' I said firmly.

She came with me.

We walked rapidly down the deserted streets in the crisp early morning air, our breath visible as puffs of white vapour.

'You should have put on a cloak, Ben,' said Rachel.

'Walking will warm me. I don't like the idea of you looking at a corpse.'

'It's my investigation,' she squeezed my hand in reassurance. 'Or, at least, *our* investigation.'

As we neared Herod's palace golden rays of sunlight touched the trees and buildings, casting long shadows across the road.

The main doors of the palace were not yet open and the night guard was still on duty.

'Ben Bartholomew,' I said to the duty sergeant. 'Captain Cornelius is expecting me.'

'Yes, certainly, sir. The captain sent word down a few minutes ago that you were to be shown straight up.'

The giant main doors, intricately carved out of Lebanese cedar, were swung open half a metre and Rachel and I went into the echoing, empty palace foyer. One of the privates came with us, and he led the way up the sweeping staircase of white marble to the first floor.

Here was yet another foyer of echoing vastness, deserted and dim at this time of the morning. The soldier led us a short distance down a corridor that opened off the foyer, and knocked on a door.

'Come in,' called the voice of our friend Publius Cornelius.

We entered and shook hands.

'Nice to see you two again,' he said, 'even under such tragic circumstances. If you want to see the body before it's moved we'll have to leave at once. Will you wait here in my office, Rachel?'

'I've come to visit the scene of the crime,' insisted my wife firmly.

Cornelius just shrugged his shoulders, pulled on a cloak, and led the way back downstairs. This time we followed a winding corridor to the back of the palace, then crossed a courtyard, rounded a corner, and came to the palace stables.

A horse was harnessed to a chariot, ready and waiting for us.

The journey from the palace to the scene of the crime, north of the city on the Mount Carmel road, is one I would rather forget.

Cornelius' chariot was a standard issue Roman officer's light-weight one-man vehicle. As such it could carry a second person, in comfort, standing close beside the driver. It could not carry a third person in comfort. I was the third person. I was carried. I was not in comfort.

My hands were gripping either side of the narrow vehicle, and my feet were just on the platform of the chariot with my heels dangling dangerously over the rear edge. On top of which, Cornelius had clearly graduated from one of the Roman's army's Advanced Driver Courses. In other words, he drove very well but very fast. Very, very fast.

The knuckles of both my hands were white as we skidded around corners leaving a plume of dust behind us settling slowly in the still morning air.

At last Cornelius pulled on the reins as we neared a group of people by the side of the road. As I stepped down onto the ground I was pleased to be on *terra firma* again — the more firmer the less terror, as far I was concerned.

'Wasn't that exhilarating!' said Rachel, brushing her long hair back from her eyes.

'Exactly the word I would have used!' I said wryly,

and then turned my attention to the group gathered by the roadside.

Most of the group were officers of the city watch who stepped aside when they saw Cornelius approaching. Rachel and I followed our friend as he led us off the shoulder of the road, and into a deep drainage ditch several metres beyond the paved surface. In the bottom of the ditch was a figure covered by a sheet.

When I saw how slim and small the covered shape was I had to look away. I noticed that Rachel did the same.

I looked back at the road. It was a broad, paved Roman road running from Caesarea to Tyre via Ptolemais. In doing so it skirted around the base of Mount Carmel — hence its name. Where we were standing was still inside the boundaries of the Roman province of Judea: the territory of Syria began a few kilometres further on.

What was Abigail doing out here? I wondered. What was she doing this far from the city boundary?

I was roused from my speculations by Cornelius' voice.

'Ben, Rachel,' he was saying, 'this is the police surgeon, Dr Nostrum.'

We said hello and politely shook hands. It seemed that even in the neighbourhood of death, etiquette was observed.

'If you'll follow me,' said Dr Nostrum, 'I'll show you the body.'

We followed him, our feet slipping down the muddy slope of the ditch. At the bottom he leaned forward and unceremoniously whipped off the sheet.

She looked very small, and very young, and very frail. My eyes misted over and a dull, heavy weight settled in my stomach. A moment later this was replaced by anger, a hot, burning anger that was determined to catch the swine who had killed this child.

'How did she die?' I asked.

'Blow to the back of the head,' said the doctor calmly, as if lecturing a class of medical students. 'You can see here that the lower part of the parietal bone and the upper part of the occipital bone have been crushed. The indentation is an odd semi-circular shape. Perhaps I should call it a half-moon shape.'

'What sort of weapon did that?'

'None that I've ever seen before.'

'So guess for me,' I insisted. 'What sort of weapon?'

'Perhaps a rock? Perhaps a wheel detached from a vehicle? But it would have to be quite a small wheel. I really don't know, I've never seen a wound quite like this before.'

'How long has she been lying here?'

'That I am more confident about: five days at least.'

'Was she killed here?'

'Looking at the settled lividity (see that purplish discolouration under the skin?) she was moved here after death.'

'Who found her?' asked Rachel.

'This officer here,' said Dr Nostrum, indicating one of the younger city watch officers.

'How did she come to be found?'

'A drunken camel-driver stumbled across her, ma'am,' said the soldier nervously, 'and I found him when I was on my 3 a.m. patrol outside the city gates. I heard the drunk's groaning coming from the ditch, and when I investigated, well, there she was. In his drunken state he'd fallen into the ditch, and couldn't get out again, just a few metres from the corpse.'

'How could this body be here for days and not be noticed?' I asked.

'The ditch is just deep enough and just far enough from the road,' said Cornelius, 'for that not to be surprising. We've had similar cases in the past. Besides which, you'll notice there's quite a lot of mud and dirt on the body and that would have disguised it to a degree.'

'Can we remove the body now, please?' said Dr Nostrum. 'I was up early and I have an autopsy to perform.'

'Yes, go ahead,' said Cornelius.

Two men in leather aprons standing beside a mortuary cart were summoned down. They lifted the body onto a rough, wooden stretcher and carried it to where their cart stood on the crown of the road.

'Have her parents been informed yet?' asked Rachel.

Cornelius shook his head. 'I was hoping...' he said.

'Do you want us to do it?'

'Would you mind?'

'We'll go and see them, won't we, Ben?'

I agreed, and we clambered up out of the ditch and back onto the paved surface of the roadway.

With the clop of horses hooves the mortuary cart began its journey back to the city.

'Poor kid,' murmured Rachel as it moved away, 'that poor kid.'

CHAPTER 10

'Any sign of a weapon around here?' I asked Cornelius. We stood on the edge of the ditch, now empty of its corpse.

'The men have searched this area pretty thoroughly,' he replied, 'and so far found nothing that could have inflicted that particular wound.'

'Did anyone check the contents of her pockets?' asked Rachel, moving close to my side.

'I did, ma'am,' said the young officer who had found the body. 'There was nothing.'

'Nothing? You mean her pockets were completely empty?'

'That's right, ma'am. Totally empty. There was nothing at all.'

'No small change?'

'No, ma'am.'

'Not even a handkerchief?'

'Not even that, m'am.'

'How peculiar,' commented Rachel, 'how very peculiar.'

'Was she carrying any identification?' I asked.

'No, sir,' replied the young soldier. 'But I recognised her from the description of the missing girl circulated by Captain Cornelius.'

'Well, I think we've seen all we can see here,' I said.

The others nodded in agreement.

To the north the golden sunlight was catching the peak of Mount Carmel and spilling down to the lower slopes. The Mediterranean sky arcing over our heads was turning a blazing and brilliant blue, and the early morning chill was starting to vanish from the air.

'What happens next?' I asked.

'A routine investigation,' replied Cornelius. 'I will instruct the city watch officers to question everyone using this road today, particularly those farmers and merchants who travel this way regularly. Perhaps one of them saw something five days ago.'

'What sort of something?' asked Rachel.

'I am hoping,' he replied, 'that when the body was disposed of, someone noticed, and can give us a description of who they saw behaving suspiciously at this spot beside the road.'

'That won't produce anything,' I remarked. 'Whoever disposed of the body did it in the dead of night.'

'You're probably right, Ben, but sometimes routine pays off, and it has to be tried. What will you do?'

'Me? My case is over now. Abigail has been found.'

'There is one last thing you can do...' said Cornelius.

'And we will,' interrupted Rachel. 'We will break the news to her parents.'

'Thank you. I feel that I'm evading my duty as a soldier — but, if you would...?'

'Yes, of course,' said Rachel.

The ride back to the city was much easier, for me at least, than the journey out: I hitched a ride on a passing farm-cart. It was slow, but it was better than hanging on for grim death to the rear of a swaying, bouncing, high-speed chariot.

By the time I eventually got back to our apartment

it was breakfast time, and I found Rachel in the kitchen with Momma.

'When are we going to break the news to Joe and Hannah?' I asked.

'Straightaway,' said Rachel briskly. 'I've been waiting for you. Why you had to come on that farm-cart, rather than Cornelius' chariot, I can't imagine.'

'If you'd balanced on the back of that chariot, as I did, you'd imagine perfectly well!'

'Rachel told me the news,' said Momma. 'It's terrible, just terrible. That poor woman.'

'What poor woman?'

'The mother, of course! Hannah! Should I come with you and Rachel so that I can comfort her?'

'No. You stay here, Momma. This is something that Rachel and I have to do.'

'Well, wash your face, Ben darling,' said Rachel, 'and brush those straws out of your hair.'

'Straws in my hair?'

'You travel on farm-carts, you end up looking like a farmer. Clean up and we'll go straight round to the Jacobsons' house.'

It was not more than fifteen minutes later that Rachel and I were standing on the Jacobsons' front porch, knocking on the door. It was opened by the same man servant we had seen on our earlier visit, and, once again, he summoned a maid to show us into the atrium while he told his master and mistress of our arrival.

We barely had a chance to sit down on the marble bench provided for guests when Joe and Hannah hurried in.

'Have you heard something?' asked Hannah.

'What's the news?' said Joe, at the same moment.

'It's bad news, I'm afraid,' I said quietly.

'You'd better sit down, Hannah,' said Rachel.

'Is Abigail all right?'

'No, Joe, she's not,' I replied. 'Her body has been found. Apparently she's been dead for several days.'

Hannah howled like an animal in pain, and then began to sob so violently, her hands over her face, that her whole body trembled. Joe walked over and put his arms around her. She buried her face in his shoulder and they both wept.

Rachel and I looked at each other, feeling awkward and helpless.

After a time Joe released Hannah and turned back to me. 'What happened, Ben? Tell me how she died,' he said, as Rachel led Hannah to the bench to sit down.

'It was murder, Joe,' I said grimly. 'She was killed by a blow to the back of the head.'

'Could it have been an accident?'

'Perhaps. But the city watch think it was murder.'

'But who? Why? She was a good kid. She had no enemies. Why was she killed, Ben, tell me that!'

'I just wish I could, Joe. But the city watch have only just begun their investigation. We'll know eventually, but we don't know now. I'm just sorry I didn't find her in time. I feel that I've let you down.'

'Nonsense. You said she's been dead for several days?'

'That's what the police surgeon said.'

'Then she was dead even before I came to you, Ben. There was nothing you could have done to prevent this tragedy.'

'Well, Joe,' I said, patting his arm, 'perhaps Rachel and I should leave you and Hannah with each other for a while. Is there anyone you want me to tell? Are there any friends or relatives who could come and be with you for a while?'

'Thank you, Ben, but no, we'll telephone some people in a little while. Besides, you and Rachel have an investigation to get on with?'

'Investigation?'

'I want you to find Abigail's murderer for me, Ben. Will you do that?'

'That's a matter for the Roman officials. The city watch will investigate, Joe. It's not a matter for a private detective any longer.'

'But I want it to be you, Ben,' he insisted. 'I want it to be. What will the city watch do?'

'They've already begun their routine,' I explained.

'Routine! Ha! That's all they're good for is routine! No, I want Abigail's killer to be *found*! I don't want that her file should collect dust along with hundreds of other unsolved murders.'

'This is official business, Joe.'

'This is personal business — that's what this is, very personal business!' he shouted. Then more quietly he added, 'Investigate for me, Ben. Take the case. Don't let her murderer escape scot-free!'

I thought of Abigail's small and frail body lying in the ditch and, even though I knew I was buying problems, I said, 'Yeah, I'll do it for you, Joe — I'll take the case.'

'Thanks, Ben. You get on to it right now. Spare no effort, spare no expense.'

Half an hour later Rachel and I were nursing cups of cappuccino in a pizza parlour in the Forum.

'Was it wise?' asked Rachel. 'I mean, wise to tell Joe that we'd investigate Abigail's murder?'

'I just couldn't say "no," Rachel, and that's a fact.'

'So, how do we go about it? What do we do?'

'For a start I want to visit Dr Nostrum at the city mortuary — find out if he's learned anything more from his autopsy.'

'And then?'

'Then go back to the pattern we've started. If Abigail has been dead at least five days then where she went to from the city library on Tuesday is crucial. And I'm convinced the key lies in that list of pagan temples. Those are the places she was interested in, those are the places she was visiting.'

One of the nice things about being conquered by the Romans is that at least you get to eat pizza. The smell of cooking pizza is irresistible, and so it was my nostrils that prompted me to say, 'I think I'll have a pizza first, Rachel, and then we'll get started.'

'At this time of day? It's nowhere near lunchtime yet and, besides, you'll only put on weight. Anyway, how can you eat after what we've been through this morning?'

'It's comfort food! When I get stressed, I eat. Besides which, I got up very early and I missed breakfast — I'm hungry.'

'Nonsense. You just imagine you're hungry because you can smell pizza. You just tell your stomach that it's imagining things, and wait until lunchtime.'

We compromised: I settled for a mid-morning snack of garlic bread and another coffee. Then we set out for the city mortuary.

CHAPTER 11

The city morgue was a large, white mausoleum of a building with a brass plate on the front wall that read: *Memento Mori*. It gave me the shivers.

The receptionist at the front told us that Dr Nostrum was working in Dissecting Room B. I didn't like the sound of that, but we followed the directions we were given. Fortunately we found the police surgeon standing in a corridor peeling rubber gloves off his hands.

'Dr Nostrum,' I said, 'may we have a word?'

'Certainly. Come with me to my office.'

We followed him down the length of the corridor and into a spacious office.

'What can I do for you?' he asked as he scrubbed his hands in a sink in the corner of the room.

'It's about the body found on the Mount Carmel road this morning.'

'What about it?' asked the doctor, discarding the green surgical gown that covered his ordinary street clothes.

'Did the autopsy tell you anything new?'

'Should I be answering your questions?' he said, raising a quizzical eyebrow. 'Why are you asking?'

'I — er, *we* — have been employed by the dead girl's parents. Originally they asked us to find her. Now they want us to find her murderer.'

'It's a private inquiry then?'

'True, but is there any reason for you not to tell us what you've found?'

He thought for a moment about this, and then remarked, 'I suppose not. Carry on.'

'Well, cause of death to begin with: anything new there?'

'No. Death was due to a depressed fracture to the back of the skull. Nothing mysterious about that.'

'What about the time of death? Your first guess was that she had been dead at least five days.'

'Not bad for a first guess,' said Dr Nostrum, smiling in a self-congratulatory way. 'Now that I've done the autopsy I'd say six days — and I think that's pretty precise.'

'Six days? Today's Monday so that means...'

'She died last Tuesday!' interrupted Rachel.

'What's so special about last Tuesday?' asked the doctor.

'That's when she was last seen alive,' I explained.

'It fits together then, doesn't it?' said the medico, leaning back in the swivel-chair behind his desk.

'For us it makes it harder,' I complained.

'In what way?' he asked.

'If she died not long after she was last seen, we have fewer movements to trace, there will be fewer people who might have seen her, spoken to her. The puzzle is harder to crack.'

'Well, if it will make it any easier, I think I can tell you the time of day she died.'

'Can you indeed! When?'

'Shortly after lunch.'

'How can you know that?' asked Rachel.

'Partially digested sandwiches still in the gut: *ergo*, she died soon after lunch.'

'Ben!' said Rachel, grabbing my arm, 'Abigail was

seen just before lunch at the city library. So she must have died not long after leaving there.'

'Precisely,' I said. 'Dr Nostrum, thank you for your help.'

Back out on the street, standing in the dusty sunshine in front of the morgue, we stood for a moment, side by side, considering the information we now had about the time of Abigail's death.

A shout of 'Look out there!' snapped us back to reality, and we both stepped back to the edge of the road as a builder's cart, heavily laden with slabs of stone, rumbled past.

'You Carthaginian crab-brain!' bellowed the cartdriver. 'Watch where you're standin' or you'll end up flatter than a daffodil under a pyramid!'

I was about to shout back some insulting remark when Rachel said, 'Just give him the frozen torso treatment.'

'The what?' I asked.

'The cold shoulder,' she said, 'don't say anything.'

When the cart had passed and the dust settled Rachel asked, 'Where to?'

'Which temple is next on Abigail's list?' I responded.

'Let's see, it's...' said Rachel, dipping into a pocket in her robe and withdrawing Abigail's note, '. . . ah, the Nothingness Temple.'

'Right. Laconicus gave me an address, a basement address.'

'Unusual. Not many temples in basements.'

'True. So let's find this one, and see what they know about Abigail's movements last Tuesday.'

The address was down near the waterfront of Caesarea. The polyglot collection of traders who frequented the area was reflected in the bars we passed. For the Gauls there was a bar called Le Café, for the Britons one called Ye Olde Tavern, for the sailors there was a bar and grill called Flotsam and Jetsam, and for the Egyptians there was a night-club called Mummy's.

In among the wharves and jetties, coils of rope and piles of barrels, sacks of grain and bars of pig iron, these bars and taverns were usually avoided by the well-scrubbed citizens of the city. Apart, that is, from university students, who thought the place was 'colourful' and 'had character.'

The weather-beaten timber buildings that lined the waterfront often housed taverns on the ground floor, or in the basement, with warehouses and shipping offices above. The address Laconicus had given me was typical. Ropes and pulleys hung from wooden beams that protruded over the street from the upper storeys, while below a set of stone steps led to a door bearing the words: The Nothingness Temple and Coffee Bar. Rachel and I pushed open the door and stepped inside.

The place was dim, dark and almost deserted. The walls were painted black, there were plain wooden tables and chairs scattered about (also painted black), a bar at one end of the room, and a low stage at the other. On the stage was a piano and several music stands and wooden stools.

Behind the bar there was a man washing glasses, and on the stage a stout, bald man sitting on the piano stool was staring at the piano keys without moving.

'Weird,' whispered Rachel.

'Weird with a capital "W," ' I replied.

I picked up a stained menu from one of the tables. It had two printed columns: one listed toasted sandwiches and coffee, the other a variety of exotic cocktails. Across the bottom, as a kind of slogan, were the words: 'There is no meaning in the universe.'

I showed it to Rachel and she raised her eyebrows.

'Let's start with him,' I said, indicating the man in the grubby apron. Rachel nodded, and we walked up to the bar.

For what felt like several long and very silent minutes the barman ignored us. Eventually, and without looking up from his work, the man muttered, 'We're closed.'

'We didn't drop in for a drink,' I explained.

This was enough to make the barman lose interest again, and another long silence followed.

'Look,' I said, 'can you tell me who's in charge here?'

'The manager,' replied the sulk.

'Well, that's a step in the right direction. What's the manager's name?'

'Mr Skinner, of course,' he replied, looking at me as if I were a retarded three-year-old, 'Mr Jack Skinner.'

'That's terrific. Now, where can I find Mr Jack Skinner?'

'What d'ya mean "where?" That's Jack, up there,' said the barman, nodding at the man sitting motionless on the piano stool.

Rachel and I started to walk towards the stage when the barman called after us, 'You'd better not disturb him — he's composing.'

We took another look at the figure on the stage — he was just sitting there. We looked at each other, shrugged our shoulders, and continued walking.

As we got closer we got a better look at Mr Jack Skinner.

He was a fat man, not grossly fat, just chubbily fat, wearing a black roll-neck sweater and black trousers. His round head was completely bald and his skin a sickly, sunless white. In fact the only splash of colour was his beard: a small, neatly trimmed goatee that was a dull red streaked with grey. And he was wearing dark glasses — as if he expected this dark cellar to be invaded any moment by the noonday sun or blinding floodlights.

'Excuse me, Mr Skinner?' I said.

He ignored me, and continued staring at the keyboard of his piano. He was so still I wondered if he was breathing.

'Are you alright?' I asked anxiously.

'No, man!' he replied in a voice that was little more than a whisper, 'I'm not alright! I've lost it! So how can I be alright?'

'Lost it? Lost what?'

'The Moment, you dunderheaded dolt! I've lost The Moment — that one creative moment that will give me the next note of the piece I am composing.'

He turned stiffly towards me and added, 'You have no respect for creativity, have you? You are as uncool as you are uncouth. The creative moment is my *sanctum sanctorum* — not to be invaded by a defective dimwitted donkey like you. Now — vanish, man! Disappear, while I try to recapture The Moment.'

I got the impression he was a little upset.

'Look, Mr Skinner, I'm sorry if...' I began.

'Sorry? Sorry? "Sorry" does not compose music. "Sorry" does not write poetry, paint paintings or carve sculptures. "Sorry" is for morons, man. Don't lay your "sorry" on me, I ain't interested.'

'Jack...' said a soft, feminine voice from somewhere near my left shoulder. I turned around and looked: it was Rachel.

'Jack…I was so sure you'd want to help us,' she said, in her softest, warmest voice.

'And who might you be, little lady?' asked Skinner, his ill-temper seemingly forgotten.

'I'm Rachel, Jack, and I'm delighted to meet you.'

'Yes, of course you are, of course you are,' was Skinner's sibilant response.

'I'm enquiring after a girl, Jack, a girl named Abigail — seventeen years of age, very pretty, long, dark hair.'

'Abigail? Abigail? Ah yes, I remember an Abigail. An extremely pretty little thing. Square, but pretty. She visited with us here some weeks ago, as I recall.'

'What can you tell me about her, Jack?' asked Rachel gently.

'Tell you? Why nothing, man. Nothing at all. She came, she went. Nothing to tell.'

And with that he turned back towards the piano.

CHAPTER 12

That was about as much as I was prepared to put up with. I grabbed the piano lid and slammed it down hard, missing Skinner's chubby fingers by millimetres.

'Now focus your mind, Jack!' I snapped. 'Focus it on Abigail. You're going to tell me everything you can remember about her.'

'Hey! Stay cool, man, stay cool!' he replied, in his soft, whispery voice. 'What's this all about?'

'It's about a seventeen-year-old girl who went missing six days ago. This morning her body was found in a ditch on the Mount Carmel road. She was murdered. And that's why you're going to be as helpful as you can possibly be. Unless, that is, you'd rather I call in the city watch and ask a couple of the larger officers to question you?'

'I'll help, man! When did I ever say that I wouldn't help?'

'When did you last see Abigail?'

'Weeks ago, man. Like maybe three weeks? Yeah, like it was three weeks ago, not six days ago. And I know nothing about her death, so don't get heavy with me.'

'How long was she here? How often did she visit?'

'Just one night, that's all. She called in one night, stayed until closing, and then left. Never came back.'

'Did you talk to her?'

'Sure, I talked to her. Lots of people here talked to her. She was like, you know, inquisitive. Wanted to know what we were on about. So she talked to me, and the musicians, and the poets, and the artists who hang around this place every night.'

'What sort of questions did she ask?'

'Deep questions, man, really deep.'

'Such as?'

'She wanted to know what it's all about.'

'What what's all about?'

'Life, the universe, everything. She wanted to know *why* — that was her big question. Is there is any purpose? Is history going anywhere?'

'And what did you tell her?'

'I told her the truth, man. There is no purpose. There is no meaning. There is no truth. Nothing. Life is absurd, baby, just absurd, so don't try to make any sense out of it, I said. I read her some of my poetry. And the band played her some of my music.'

'What band is this?'

'They're called the Ad Hoc, Ad Infinitum, Ad Nauseam jazz band; they play here every night. Very cool. Like there's a double bass, clarinet, bongos and piano. Let me play you some of it, man. Who knows, maybe you'll dig it?'

Jack Skinner opened up the piano lid, hovered over the keys for a moment, and then began to play.

Rachel and I turned and looked at each other. And without a word we both agreed on one thing: no one ever came here for the music. There was nothing to it — just sparse, occasional notes: splink, splank, splonk — that's all.

'You like it, man? You dig it?' whispered the extremely cool Mr Skinner.

'Very nice, I'm sure,' said Rachel. 'But did Abigail dig it?'

'No way! She was so square she was cubic. She had no soul, man, no soul.'

'Thanks for your time, Mr Skinner,' I said. 'You've been very helpful.'

Rachel and I had walked some blocks from The Nothingness Temple and Coffee Shop before either of us spoke.

'That's not a philosophy of life,' I muttered, 'that's a scream of despair!'

'Poor Abigail,' said Rachel, 'she must have been very confused, or desperate, to spend a whole evening exploring that view of the world.'

'Once you say: "There is no meaning in the universe" — which is what Skinner says — then you get absolutely nowhere.'

'Hmmm,' said Rachel, nodding thoughtfully.

'But there is a paradox, a built-in contradiction there.'

'How so?'

'Well, in order to be a practising "nothingness" person you have to deny *something*. Jack Skinner is being supercool denying the meaning that other people can see in the universe.'

'Like a parasite?'

'Exactly. In order to create a work of art (however weird) there must be some structure, some meaning, that is being rebelled against.'

'And if someone *really* believed in nothing — no purpose, no meaning, no direction, no truth — what then? Suicide?'

'Yes. Certainly the suicide of all that is recognisably human: the hunger for meaning, value, significance, dignity, truth. There are no easy answers, but to pretend there are no answers at all doesn't make the questions go away.'

'Oh,' said Rachel with a shudder, 'that place is like a thick fog; a sickly, unhealthy swamp.'

'Let's do what Abigail did then; let's turn our back on it and move on.'

Since we were in the waterfront district I proposed that we drop in on Petronius Laconicus, to see if he'd managed to turn up any leads.

We found Laconicus slumped over his corner desk, his quill dangling loosely from his fingers, looking more dejected than ever.

'Morning, sunshine!' I said.

'Oh, it's you again,' he murmured. 'But this time accompanied by a beautiful damsel. Make the introductions, Bartholomew.'

'This is my wife Rachel. Sweetheart, this is the well-known drunken hack Petronius Laconicus.'

'My pleasure,' said Rachel.

'No, you are quite wrong. The pleasure is all mine,' growled Laconicus, an apology for a smile slowly spreading over his gloomy countenance.

'What is the reason for all this gloom anyway?' I asked, as Rachel and I pulled up chairs and sat down.

'I told you I had to do the chariot-racing tips for last weekend's paper?'

'Yes. The regular guy was away or something.'

'That's right. Well, it turned out that my tipping was more accurate than his, and now they're talking about sacking him and making me do it all the time.'

'But you know nothing about chariot-racing!'

'I told them that. I explained that I just stabbed a dagger while blindfolded into a piece of papyrus to pick the winners.'

'And what did they say to that?'

'They are very superstitious (like all Romans) and they said I had invented a wonderful new method of divination! Can you believe that? And, as if that were not bad enough, now...huh!' Laconicus snorted derisively.

'Now — what?' I asked.

'Now they have me filling in on the social column while the lady who usually writes it is away having a rest cure at the Dead Sea Health Spa.'

'So the mad social whirl is not your world, I take it?' asked Rachel.

'I'm usually on the police beat,' explained Laconicus. 'What do I care about who's having cocktails with Governor Pilate, or who Lady Claudia has been twittering at lately?'

'I take your point,' I said. 'But tell me this: have you got any information for me yet? Something substantial that I can get my dentures into?'

'Ah, that is an equine of another hue. Because of all the work they have loaded onto me I have only made a few enquiries so far.'

'I'll come back later then,' I said, starting to rise.

'Don't be so hasty. I said "a few enquiries" — not none. And I have uncovered what may turn out to be your best lead.'

'Tell me more.'

'It's a man named Vacuus — I don't know his real name, but that's the nickname everyone knows him by.'

'Vacuus — okay, what about him?'

'He's a big man (two metres tall, two metres wide) was a professional wrestler when he was younger. But he became a religious maniac of sorts. Went from temple to temple taking up each new fad, each new religion, as it rolled into town. He hung around the

82

temples so much he was often employed as an occasional odd-job man for them. Still is. He's a big, dumb ox of a man.'

'I get the picture: he's no Aristotle.'

'He's a shekel short of a denarius, if you get my drift. But despite that, he knows every temple in town, and every racket they're into. If you question him carefully you might find out something useful.'

'What are his *bona fides* like?'

'His "*bona*" is not too good and his "*fides*" lack authority. But if you keep your wits about you, you might learn something from his answers.'

'Sounds worth trying. Where can I find him?'

'I couldn't find a home address, and the only work he does is on an odd-job basis, so there's no work address. But there is a bar he hangs around a lot. A place called the Ipso Vino bar and grill. Run by a man named Maximus — another nick-name: he got it from the size of the drinks he serves. Try there.'

'I will. Many thanks, old chum. And good luck with the social column.'

'You two clear off then. I've got to put pen to parchment and try to get some work done.'

As Rachel and I stepped out of the building a grubby young urchin — one of the human street-rats of the waterfront — ran up to me, thrust a piece of papyrus into my hand, and ran off again. It all happened so fast that I did not see where he had come from, and before I could recover he had disappeared up a narrow alley like a rat up a drain-pipe.

'What was that all about?' asked Rachel.

'Some sort of message service, I presume,' I replied, holding up the papyrus.

'Well, let's hear the message then.'

I opened the note and read the four-word message: 'You have been warned.'

'Another one,' said Rachel quietly. 'Let me have a closer look at that.'

I handed over the note.

'These words have been written with a very strange black ink. Perhaps that will help you track down the source?'

'That's not ink, my love. That's dried blood!'

CHAPTER 13

'Dried blood? Yuk!' said Rachel, hurriedly handing the note back to me.

'Yes. The note was written in fresh blood, I would guess, and it's gone black as it's dried.'

'The blood is part of the message, isn't it?'

'Like the dagger in our front door, yes. Perhaps from now on you'd better leave this investigation to me, sweetheart.'

A look of cold bronze came into Rachel's eyes as I spoke those words.

'No way!' she said firmly. 'We are in this together. Where you go, I go.'

'Except to the Ipso Vino bar and grill tonight to talk to Maximus and track down Vacuus.'

'That's tonight. It's only the middle of the afternoon — time enough to visit the next temple on the list.'

With that, Rachel pulled Abigail's list out of the belt that was tied around her robe, and ran her eye down the slip of paper: 'The Temple of the Golden Eye.'

Our journey took us through the university district of Caesarea. The streets seemed to be full of students in short togas chatting up other students in short togas. All the buildings had signs advertising their educational services. We passed the Kudos Academy of Rhetoric, the Lapsus Memoriae Essay Writing Service, and a dozen others.

The Golden Eye temple was impressively modern in appearance. You'll notice that I didn't call it attractive — just modern. It looked as though it had been put together by a child with a set of building blocks: large, concrete building blocks.

Once inside the sliding glass front doors we found ourselves in a lobby where bland, fawn-coloured carpet blended in with even blander, cream-coloured walls. The only break in the monotony was a sign saying 'Entrance' above an arrow that pointed to a plain, white door.

Pushing open the door we discovered a short corridor lined with floor-to-ceiling mirrors. At the far end the corridor turned to the right, and then a few metres further on, to the left, then to the right again.

'What a peculiar way to enter a building,' complained Rachel.

'Peculiar is being polite,' I remarked. 'Crazy is more like it.'

'A corridor that twists and turns...'

'And all of it lined with floor-to-ceiling mirrors. What does it mean?'

'And when are we going to get to the end of it?' asked Rachel, then she stopped and turned towards me. 'It couldn't be, could it?'

'Couldn't be what?' I asked.

'Are we going around in circles?'

'This is the way into the temple, Rachel. So we are not going around in circles, we are going into the temple. Eventually.'

'If I'm right, it could take us some time.'

'How so? The building's not so big. We should be

out of this winding corridor and into the main part of the temple in the next few steps.'

'Yes, we should be — but we won't!'

And she was right.

From the outside the building had not looked to be so very big, but we were trudging back and forth through a twisting, turning corridor that seemed to go on for kilometres.

'Okay,' I said at last, 'I give up. What's going on here?'

'It must be a mirror maze,' said Rachel. 'You know, the sort of thing you see at carnivals.'

'That makes no sense. Why would the main public entrance to a temple be through a mirror maze?'

'I don't know why. Perhaps it reflects their beliefs?'

'Pun intended?'

'I'm afraid so. Sorry about that.'

'So stop making puns already, and find a way out of this.'

'I think the trick will be to push against these full-length mirrors set into the walls. Some of them will be doors.'

So we tried every mirror and, sure enough, we found that quite a number of them were doors. But that was just the start. Most of the doors just led to more mirror-lined corridors, and kept us going around in the same old circles.

'I've got an idea,' said Rachel.

'I'm glad,' I said, 'because I have run out of ideas and patience.'

'With a lot of mazes the way out can be found by constantly taking turns in the same direction.'

'What do you mean?'

Rachel led the way, and at every point where a

mirrored door gave us a choice of direction she chose to turn to the right. After ten minutes it became obvious that we were still getting nowhere.

'Okay, we'll try the other direction then,' said Rachel with determination.

This time we turned left at every intersection, and, after only about two minutes of walking we pushed against one of the mirror doors set into the walls, and found ourselves stepping out into the main part of the temple.

Set into the front wall, directly ahead of us, was the symbol of the temple: a giant eye fashioned out of gold.

The only furniture was a circle of stackable chairs, arranged as if for a tutorial or discussion group. One of these chairs was occupied by a man who was scribbling furiously on a writing pad that was balanced on his knee.

'Excuse me,' I said. He ignored us.

'Hello there,' I added, a little louder. He ignored us more loudly.

He was a short, squat man with close-cropped greying hair, wearing glasses and a crumpled grey suit.

'Good afternoon,' said Rachel.

At the sound of a woman's voice he put down his pen and looked up. He took off his reading glasses and looked up at Rachel intently for a minute.

'Can I help you?' he asked, after completing his inspection.

'We're looking for whoever is in charge here.'

'You've found him. John Paulson is the name. How can I help you?'

'We have a few questions.'

'Perhaps you should come to one of our beginners' discussion groups — every Monday night at eight.'

'Not those sort of questions.'

'What sort then?'

'Abigail Jacobson, a seventeen-year-old girl, visited here recently.'

'Abigail who?'

'Jacobson.'

'Never heard of her,' he said, turning back to his writing.

'Perhaps you'll recognise her picture,' said Rachel, pulling out the photograph Joe had provided.

Paulson studied this for a moment, and then said thoughtfully, 'A pretty girl. I should have liked to have known her better.'

'She was here then?'

'Oh, yes. Certainly. She came to a number of lectures and study groups.'

'When was the last time you saw her?'

'Perhaps two weeks ago. Something like that, I would think. Why are you asking all these questions?'

'She has been murdered. We are trying to re-trace her movements in the weeks leading up to her death.'

'I see. Very well then, I will help you.' So saying, he placed his writing pad and pen to one side, and turned to face us squarely. 'Ask your questions.'

He had a thick foreign accent (Gaulish, I think) and a face lined by a life of worry.

'When she came here,' began Rachel, 'she was on some sort of quest.'

'Correct,' muttered Paulson, 'the quest for truth. This quest I am not unacquainted with. I told her to make her own truth.'

'What else did you tell her.'

'Before I talked, I listened. She told me her story. She had started, she said, at The Temple of the Great Clockmaker, had gone on to The Temple that Matters and then The Nothingness Temple and Coffee Bar. I told her I had made a somewhat similar journey in my youth, so I could relate to her quest.'

'Had she found what she was looking for in her quest?'

'No! Of course not! It is not to be found in any of those places. Nevertheless, the journey she took is the journey of an intelligent mind. She started with The Clockmaker: with the idea of a God who made the world but is not involved in it. But if God is not involved, why bother assuming that God is even there? This leads one on to The Temple that Matters. But materialism fails to satisfy the human need for purpose. If matter is all there is, then the world is absurd and meaningless. Which, of course, is what they say they believe at The Nothingness Temple.'

'A logical progression,' I commented.

'Indeed,' said Paulson, as if encouraging the class dunce. 'But who can live with complete meaninglessness? No one can! The ones who don't commit suicide at The Nothingness Temple can only remain sane by being inconsistent: by acting, when they cook meals or paint pictures or make love, as if there really is some meaning somewhere.'

'Yes, we have re-traced Abigail's journey up to this point.'

'And this is where it leads to: this place here!' said Paulson emphatically, slapping his thigh loudly to make his point, and sending echos rolling around the room.

'Here we *make* meaning. We act. We act passionately. We *choose* to have meaning in our lives.'

'But what do you do?' asked Rachel. 'What actions do you perform so passionately?'

'*Any* actions! That is the point!'

'I'm afraid I don't...'

'I will explain. Only very briefly, but I will explain,' said Paulson with a tired sigh, as if he were talking to three-year-olds with room-temperature IQs.

CHAPTER 14

'Before I begin,' said Paulson, 'look into the eye.'

As he spoke he gestured towards the giant human eye, sculptured out of gold, that adorned the wall in front of us.

'Look…where?' I asked.

'Into it! Into it! Walk up to the eye and look into it!'

I approached the golden sculpture, and as I got closer I saw that the pupil was hollow.

'Into here?' I asked. John Paulson nodded furiously in response.

I leaned forward, until my face was almost touching the sculpture, and peered intently into the hollow pupil. Then I pulled back in shock. Staring back at me, out of the centre of that eye, was — me! It took only a second to realise that at the back of the hollowed-out pupil was a mirror, but the first glance succeeded in startling me.

'You see?' asked Paulson.

'See what?' I asked cautiously.

'Huh! Idiot! See what it's all about?'

'We would appreciate it if you would explain, Mr Paulson,' said Rachel soothingly.

'I can see that I will have to. Sit down here in front of me, so that I don't have to crane my neck.'

Rachel and I sat down, and John Paulson began: 'We do not live in one world: we live in two distinct worlds. Firstly, there is the objective, external, material world of which those materialists at The Temple that Matters give a perfectly adequate account. And secondly, there is the subjective, conscious, self-aware world of the human being.'

I glanced at Rachel as if to say 'So what?', but Paulson's snapped command of 'Pay attention!' brought my eyes swiftly back to him. Then he continued: 'Only human beings are self-conscious and self-determinant. Every item in the material, or objective, world is what it is: salt is salt, trees are tree, ants are ant. Only humans decide, subjectively, what they are: they decide to be heroic or cowardly, generous or selfish, hard-working or lazy. Men make themselves.'

'And women,' interrupted Rachel.

'Eh?'

'And women. Men *and women* make themselves. At least, according to your philosophy they do.'

'Quite so. Now, where was I? Ah, yes. Each person is totally free as regards their nature and destiny. Each of us is the king of our own subjective world.'

'So the philosophies of all the other temples are quite wrong?' I asked.

'Just listen! The objective world is absurd and meaningless — a foreign land in which we subjective human beings dwell as aliens. The people at The Nothingness Temple are quite right about that. However, the authentic person must revolt against the absurd and meaningless universe — and create his own value and his own meaning.'

Paulson paused significantly. There was a long and heavy silence.

'That's it?' I asked.

'Of course that's not it! That's a mere glimpse of

an outline of "it" — as you call it. But it's about all that you can cope with! If you want to know more come back on a Monday night — beginner's night!'

With that, John Paulson snatched up his pad and pen, and stumped off across the hall, to exit through a back door.

'What a grouch!' said Rachel.

'About as charming as a North African plague rat,' I agreed.

I wandered around the echoing hall. It felt very bare and empty. Lying on one of the chairs was a paperback book. I picked it up and read the title: *Alice Through the Looking Glass — The Annotated Edition*. In the back of the book was a slip of paper containing the times for various philosophical and literary discussion groups at the temple.

'There's nothing more for us here,' said Rachel with a shudder. 'This place makes me feel cold.'

'You're right,' I said, 'Let's go.'

Getting out was easier than getting in, since we now knew the rule: to get out of the mirror maze you just keep turning to the right. So within a few minutes we were outside The Temple of the Golden Eye, back on the busy street that was now bathed in the reddish glow of sunset.

'Would that have satisfied Abigail, do you think?' I asked, as we battled our way through the bustling crowd of pedestrians, camels, carts and heavily laden donkeys.

'The idea of making your own truth? I suspect not,' replied Rachel.

'Why not?'

'Well, I've been asking myself why Abigail was on this quest for truth, and my best guess is that she was lonely.'

'Lonely?'

'Yes. She was at an age when loneliness is not uncommon. She was an only child. She was a very shy, quiet girl. I think she was lonely.'

'Hmmm. You could be right.'

'And John Paulson's ideas offer nothing for loneliness. What he is trying to do is to transcend "nothingness," the hopeless feeling that the universe is meaningless. Yet he fails to provide anything outside the subjective individual. There is no reference point outside the individual person; there is no point of connection outside of me — at least, according to his ideas.'

'On top of which, the objective world keeps intruding. Especially in the form of death. Death puts an end to whatever meaning the individual might have created for him or herself.'

'Yes. What you end up with, if you follow those ideas, is the lonely self. The lonely self that lives seventy or eighty years and then ceases to exist. It does not escape "nothingness," hopelessness, at all — it just puts a mask on it for a while, that's all.'

We had now reached the Forum, the vast, open market square that stood plumb in the middle of Caesarea.

With the sun setting and the chilly evening sea breezes blowing up from the harbour, most of the stall holders had already packed up for the day, and the few remaining were in the process of pulling down their stalls and packing away their produce. The milling crowds of shoppers who filled the Forum mid-morning and mid-afternoon were now largely gone, and Rachel and I could walk briskly across the wide open spaces.

Behind me I heard the rattle of wooden wheels on

cobblestones but thought nothing of it until a voice from the other side of the square bellowed loudly: 'Watch out!'

I turned around, and there, just metres behind us, and bearing down on us like an arrow from a bow, was a speeding chariot.

I grabbed Rachel and thrust her as hard as I could to one side. Then I leapt after her.

The chariot thundered past, missing my legs by millimetres.

It was so close I could see the wide eyes and flaring nostrils of the horse; so close it tugged my cloak into the wind it whipped up; so close it almost gave me splinters as it passed.

I hurried over to where I had flung Rachel onto the cobblestones.

'Are you all right?' I asked, crouching down.

'I...I think so...' she murmured.

'You two hurt?' called one of the late stall-holders as he ran across towards us.

'We're okay — I think,' I said, rising to my feet. 'What happened?'

'I was packing up for the day,' puffed out the short, bald little stall-holder, 'when I looked up and saw that lunatic charioteer heading straight for you. Well, all I could do was to call out a warning.'

'Thank you for that, stranger,' I said. 'You probably saved our lives.'

'You betcha. If you hadn't got out of the way you two would've been mincemeat by now.'

'Thank you again. Can you stand up, honey?' I added, turning to Rachel. 'Here, give me your hand.'

'There's no serious damage...I think,' said Rachel, wincing with pain as she stood up slowly, 'but I will have some lovely bruises tomorrow.'

'That's my fault, I'm afraid, for throwing you out of the way quite so hard.'

'Don't apologise, my love — I'm still alive and there are no bones broken.'

'Well, if you folks are okay,' said the stall-holder, 'I'll get back to my packing up.'

'We're just fine,' I replied, 'And thank you again…'

'Ventriculus, that's the name. I run the bakery stall on the south side of the Forum.'

'Tell me, Ventriculus, did you see who was driving the chariot? What did he look like?'

'Gee, I don't know. He sort of had his cloak wrapped up high around his face.'

'From what you saw, did it look as though he was deliberately trying to run us down?'

'Well…look, it's hard to say. I mean, if the city watch start asking me questions, I guess I'd say that the driver was drunk. Either that or a little non compos mentis.'

'So he was driving like a drunk or a madman?'

'Exactly. You two still look pretty shaken up. Look, come over here with me to my stall: we can wash the dust off your cuts and grazes.'

At Ventriculus' stall the little baker found a jug of water and a clean cloth, and gently sponged the dust and dirt off Rachel's superficial wounds. Then he gave me the cloth and I rinsed off my own grazed knees and elbows.

While I was doing that he went to the back of his stall and fetched out a basket of small loaves.

'Here, take these,' he said. 'It's the end of the day so I won't sell them now, and by tomorrow they'll be stale. Take them with my compliments — to cheer you up after the accident. A baker's dozen of my best buns.'

'Thank you kindly,' said Rachel. 'A baker's dozen, you say? Thirteen?'

'Eleven! Never trust a Caesarean baker!' replied Ventriculus, and then he laughed at his own joke.

CHAPTER 15

'Ben,' asked Rachel, as we hobbled home through the darkening streets, 'was that really an accident?'

'You mean was someone putting some muscle behind those threats?'

'Exactly.'

'The answer is, my love, that I really don't know.'

'But you suspect, don't you?'

'I'm not sure...but...'

'Come on. Tell me what you really think.'

'I really think you should have nothing more to do with this investigation!'

'Then you don't believe it was an accident!' cried Rachel triumphantly. 'I knew it!'

'All right. I'll tell what I think was happening back there. For a start I don't think it was a serious attempt on our lives.'

'You don't?'

'Certainly not. If that driver had wanted to kill us he easily could have. He missed — narrowly — because that's what he was trying to do.'

'Meaning...what exactly?'

'Meaning that we have just had another warning. No note this time, but the warning is even clearer.'

We walked the rest of the way in silence. From time to time I glanced at Rachel. A particularly sombre and thoughtful expression darkened her pretty face.

Our arrival at our front door coincided with the arrival of a visitor: Philip, the young man we had met at synagogue on Saturday.

'You two have been in the wars,' were his opening words. 'What's happened?'

'A slight accident, that's all', I said.

'A close encounter with a fast-moving horse and chariot,' added Rachel with a wry smile.

'Are you all right?'

On being assured that we were both fine, Philip continued: 'I was just popping in to invite you two to my place next Sunday morning. I'm getting together all the Christians I can find in Caesarea.'

'What do you mean "all the Christians"?' asked Rachel. 'We thought we were the only two — until you arrived.'

'Well, there are a few more. And some interested enquirers. I thought we'd get together for a meal, some fellowship, Bible study and prayer. Can you two come?'

We assured him that we would be there with bells on, he gave us his address, and hurried on to his next appointment.

Rachel and I opened our front door and trudged wearily upstairs, all our muscles aching with the effort.

'Eeeeh! What's happened?' shrieked Momma when she saw us. 'My poor Benjamin! My poor Rachel! Who has tried to kill you? I'll kill him, whoever it is!'

'Just relax, Momma,' I said soothingly. 'Don't get homicidal.'

'I'm not getting homicidal! But I'll kill whoever did this to you!'

'We're all right, Momma, honestly we are,'

insisted Rachel. 'There was a bit of a road accident, that's all.'

'More than a bit!' snorted Momma. 'A full bit and bridle, more like it. Tell me what happened.'

'It was in the Forum,' said Rachel with a sigh, 'There was this charioteer, and we didn't see him until the last minute.'

'And so you nearly got run down? Terrible! Terrible! And this charioteer you didn't see, I take it he also didn't see you?'

'I guess so, Momma.'

'I guess not!' said Momma, putting her hands on her hips. 'I guess this paluka had something to do with that threatening note that was stuck to the door.'

'We're both all right,' I insisted, 'and that's all that matters.'

'First you're warned, then you're attacked. I should wait until you are murdered in your bed maybe? I'm putting my foot down. In fact, I'm putting both feet down: you two are having nothing more to do with this case.'

'Momma...'

'I'll put a notice on the front door downstairs saying you have given up the case!'

'And you imagine that will put a spoke in his chariot?'

'Chariots have already got spokes. I don't know what you're talking about, Benjamin. And as for you, Rachel, I don't know what you're doing allowing my Benjamin to takes risks like this.'

'Don't start blaming Rachel now...' I interrupted, but Momma paid no attention, she just ploughed on:

'You should have a nice quiet law practice, that's what you should have. You should not be back detecting when there is a homicidal maniac running amuck.'

'Momma, you are getting overwrought. Just calm down. Sit down on the sofa while I explain one or two things to you.'

To my amazement Momma did as she was told and sat down on the sofa.

'In the first place,' I continued, 'you, yourself, said it was a good idea for me to take this case. No, don't interrupt! In the second place, Rachel and I have now made a commitment to Abigail's parents and we are not pulling out. And in the third place, if you are so worried about what is happening you should go back to Jerusalem and stop worrying and look after Poppa.'

There was a long silence after I finished this speech. Then Momma said: 'I'll make dinner then.' And she did.

When she had gone into the kitchen Rachel came over to where I was standing, threw her arms around me, and hugged me tightly.

'She worries about us, that's why she talks like that,' said my darling wife.

'Hold on! Yesterday you were the one who wanted her to go back to Jerusalem.'

'Sshh! She'll hear you. I think it's sweet that she worries so much.'

Women! You marry them, you love them, but who can understand them? Not Ben Bartholomew, that's for sure!

A fine, warm, Mediterranean rain was falling when I left the house after dinner, and the sidewalks were gleaming under the street lamps and reflecting back the flashes of the neon signs.

Directly overhead was the flashing sign of one of

Caesarea's most famous nightclubs, The Bacchus. Next to it was a sign advertising Achilles' Medicinal Brandy with its famous slogan, 'Achilles' Heals.'

Passing through the business district — dark and shut at this time of night — I saw the huge revolving sign of the Midas Credit Union. In the distance was a flashing sign advertising the famous Nectar brand of beer.

Soon I was in the waterfront district and passing dingy bars with names like The Mermaid, The Typhoon and The Lotus-eaters. It was not yet midnight and already there were drunks lying in doorways and staggering along the street, giving voice to raucous song.

I found the Ipso Vino bar and grill halfway down a narrow, dark alley. Inside, the oil lamps flickered low and small groups sat around dingy tables, playing cards and drinking rum as fast as they could get it down.

Above the bar was a sign advertising 'nectar and ambrosia' — that usually meant third-rate booze and sixth-rate food.

'I'm looking for Maximus,' I said, walking up to the bar.

'Who wants him?' asked the skinny, weasel-faced barman.

'The name's Bartholomew — Ben Bartholomew,' I replied as I let a denarius fall with a tinkle onto the bar. 'Laconicus sent me.'

Scooping up the coin with a movement too swift for the human eye to follow, the little barman said, 'I'm Maximus. What do you want to know?'

'There's a man named Vacuus. I'm told he's a friend of yours. Where can I find him?'

'You're in luck, mister. He's over there, in his

usual corner.' He nodded his head in the direction of the furthest, darkest corner as he spoke.

'Thanks,' I said, and turned to walk away from the bar.

'Hey!' he called out from behind me, 'don't you wanna buy a drink?'

'I don't think my stomach could...' I began.

'Sure you wanna buy a drink,' he said. 'In fact, you wanna buy two drinks.'

'Ah, yes. Of course I do. I'd just forgotten for a moment, that's all. What's our friend drinking tonight?'

Maximus splashed small amounts of hundred-proof rum into two tiny glasses, then charged me twice the going rate.

'Thanks heaps,' I said, and then turned and carried the drinks to the corner where Vacuus sat.

'Can I join you?' I asked when I reached his table.

'Huh?' he replied.

'Can I buy you a drink?'

'Huh?'

In the dim light that penetrated this corner I could make out a huge ox of a man. His shoulders were as wide as a doorway, his arms were like Corinthian columns, and his legs were so long that his feet stuck out from the other side of the table.

'You say somethin', mister?' he rumbled at me.

'I said: may I sit down, and may I buy you a drink?'

'Uh. I guess so.'

I sat down.

'Your name Vacuus?' I asked.

'Huh?'

(As well as being the size of an ox, this man was as dumb as an ox!)

'Your name Vacuus?' I repeated.

'Yeah. Who are you?'

'The name is Bartholomew — Ben Bartholomew. Laconicus said you might be able to help me.'

'Laconicus? Oh, yeah. The reporter guy.'

'That's right — him. He said you might be able to help me.'

Suddenly Vacuus started to laugh, a slow, deep laugh that rumbled like a small earthquake.

'Me? Help you?' he laughed again, 'I guess maybe I can.'

The laughter stopped. And what it was all about I had no idea.

'Can you tell me something about some of the temples in Caesarea?'

'Temples? Yeah. I might be able to do that'

CHAPTER 16

I had brought with me the list that Rachel and I had recovered from Abigail's room. I pulled it out of a fold in my toga and pushed it across the table towards him.

'Uh. The light's bad here,' he said squinting at the list and then pushing it back again. 'You read it to me.'

I read the list to him.

'You know those temples?' I asked.

'Most of 'em,' he replied.

'Which don't you know?'

'Read the list again.'

I read the list again.

'The last one. Uh, yeah. Just the last one on the list. That's the only one I don't know.'

'That's The Haunted Temple?'

'Never come across it.'

This Haunted Temple had me puzzled: why had no one heard of it?

'But the others you have come across?' I asked.

'Uh, sure.'

'Tell me about them.'

'What do you want to know?' rumbled the ox.

'For a start, are they honest? Or are any of them con jobs?' I asked.

'That lot on your list there, mister, they're pretty honest. The Nothingness Temple and Coffee Bar rips off the university students who think it's smart to be seen there, I guess. And The Temple of the Great Clockmaker is mainly for guys who wanna make business contacts. But they're pretty honest. As temples go. Now I could tell ya about one or two others that got these really rich scams going. There's one that...'

'But this lot here,' I interrupted, 'are genuine? Sincere?'

He laughed at the word, and again the table, the chairs, the whole corner of the room, seemed to vibrate with his laughter.

'Maybe that ain't such a bad word after all,' he said when the laughter subsided. 'If they are wrong, they are sincerely wrong.'

Then he grinned, clearly delighted with what he had just said.

'Have another drink,' I said, pushing the second small rum across the table (there was no way I was going to expose my stomach to Maximus' rotgut).

'Why you askin' me these questions?' said Vacuus, suddenly suspicious.

'There's a girl who's been murdered. Her name is Jacobson. Her father has hired me to find her killer, so I'm trying to trace her movements shortly before she died. And she visited a lot of temples in the time leading up to her murder.'

'Uh huh. So?'

'So you know a lot of the temples in this town, and I thought you might be able to give me a lead on her.'

'Nope. Not me. Never seen her.'

'Could she have come to any harm at any of these temples?'

'Uh, no. No harm. Not at those temples.'

'How can you be so sure?'

'Those ones? Those are harmless temples. Namby-pamby stuff. You oughta be at the Mithras Temple when they're killing the bull. Or at the Venus Temple...oh boy!'

'So her murder had nothing to do with temples she was visiting?'

'Uh, yeah. Sure. Nothin' at all.'

'And you never saw her?'

'Never set eyes on the kid.'

'Never heard her name mentioned?' I persisted.

'Nobody never talked about no Abigail Jacobson to me.'

Crash!

Suddenly a bar stool came flying through the air, landing on our table, and cracking it in two. I spun around to find that one of the card games had turned into a fight. Within seconds the room had erupted into a wild, brawling mêlée.

I leaped up, pressed my back against the wall, and made myself as thin as possible, to avoid the flying punches and flying furniture. Already half the chairs in the room had been turned into matchwood. I'd heard of convertible furniture, but this was ridiculous.

'Huh!' snorted Vacuus, 'when they play cards they always cheat, and they always fight. I fix this.'

He lumbered awkwardly to his feet. Standing fully upright I realised what a giant of a man he was. He pushed the remnants of our table to one side and waded into the fight.

Vacuus grabbed two of the largest, most drunken brawlers, tucked them under each arm like parcels ready for the post, and carried them outside. A moment later he returned, empty-handed, and repeated the procedure on two more of the cardplayers swinging drunken punches.

Within minutes that big, dumb ox of a man had emptied the bar of its most violent brawlers, and the rest soon forgot the fight and got back to serious drinking. Apart from a sour-faced Maximus sweeping up the wreckage it was as if the fight had never happened.

Then I realised what service Vacuus provided for Maximus: in return for free drinks he bounced the brawlers.

I slipped quietly away while Vacuus and Maximus were still cleaning up, and made my way across town, back to our tiny apartment.

A sea breeze was blowing in from the harbour, and I pulled my cloak tightly around my shoulders as I hurried, head down against the swirling wind, through the dark streets of the sleeping city.

As I walked, my mind buzzed with what I had learned from Vacuus. And with a problem that was starting to haunt me: The Haunted Temple — why had no one heard of it? If Vacuus was telling the truth and the other temples on Abigail's list were harmless, was it at The Haunted Temple that she met her death? And was it unknown because it was some sort of secret 'underground' temple?

My head was still buzzing with questions as I climbed into bed and cuddled up to the warm body of my sleeping wife.

Rachel stirred in her sleep, 'Wha' time is it?' she asked without opening her eyes.

'Very late. Go back to sleep.'

'Wha' you find out?'

'I'll tell you in the morning. Goodnight, sweetheart.'

'Goo'night.'

When I awoke in the morning I found that Rachel and Momma were already up and breakfast was cooked.

'Well, tell me what you found out,' said Rachel as I attacked my morning eggs and orange juice.

So I told her. I repeated the conversation with Vacuus word for word.

'Interesting,' she commented.

'What do you make of it?' I asked.

'I'm not sure I believe him, for a start. Or trust him, for that matter.'

'Exactly. And if you'd seen him, you'd feel that distrust even more strongly. On the other hand, I don't know whether he really knows something, or is just a shady character who doesn't want to encourage any investigation into the temples of Caesarea.'

'Did you get the impression that he was trying to dodge any of your questions?'

'It's hard to tell, because he answered so slowly. It may be that he was being cagey. Or maybe he is as thick as a wart on a leper's toe.'

'That's a horrible expression, Benjamin,' said Momma. 'You shouldn't talk like that.'

'Personally I favour the latter,' I concluded, ignoring Momma's interruption.

'So where does that leave us?'

'No change of plans. I don't trust Vacuus, and I still think we should treat the temples as being under suspicion.'

'I agree. The One Temple is next on the list.'

'I have the address, and I seem to remember it was fashionable several seasons ago.'

'The latest fad is somewhere else now, I take it?'

'Yes, The Inner Temple is the one the glitterati go to these days.'

'Let's go then. We'll be back later, Momma.'

'Wait on, Rachel,' I said, 'there's something I'd like to do first. In the light of yesterday's "warning"...'

'Almost being run down by a chariot, you mean!'

'That's what I mean. In the light of that, I want to ring Cornelius to see if some sort of official protection might be available.'

I had the usual difficulty getting through the Palace switchboard, but eventually I heard our friend's voice on the end of the line.

'Captain Cornelius speaking.'

'It's Ben. I'm calling to ask for a favour.'

'If I can help I will.'

As briefly as possible I ran through the series of warnings and threats that Rachel and I had received: the note knifed to the front door, the note thrust into my hand by the urchin, and the near miss by the cheerful charioteer.

'Not very pleasant, I grant you,' said Cornelius, 'but where do I come in?'

'Do Rachel and I (and Momma for that matter — she's staying with us at the moment) qualify for official protection? Would it be possible to have an armed soldier on duty outside our place for the new few nights?'

'Hhhmm. That might be a little difficult. If it was up to me I'd approve it in an instant. But I hold a modest place in a big military machine and the decision would have to be made several levels over my head. I'll try but...'

At that a moment there was a muffled roar out in the street.

'Hold the line, Cornelius — something's just happened outside!'

I dropped the phone and rushed downstairs.

As I flung open the front door I was confronted by a blast of heat and a roar of flames. The whole front of the building seemed to be on fire.

I leaped over the flames, sprinted to the well in the courtyard, filled two buckets and ran back. By the time I had flung the water onto the fire I found that half the neighbourhood was behind me — also carrying buckets.

The fire was much smaller than the roar and crackle of the flames had suggested, and the fire was down to embers with half a dozen buckets, and completely out with a dozen.

Rachel hurried to my side and together we examined the damage: a lot of serious charring, paint blackened and peeling, but no structural damage at all.

Lying on the ground near the front wall were the fragments of a terracotta pot. I picked up one and sniffed it. Paraffin! Someone had flung a jug of paraffin against our front wall and then thrown a match into it.

Then I remembered Cornelius waiting patiently on the phone upstairs, and ran up the stairs two at a time.

'You still there?' I puffed, as I picked up the phone.

'Still here,' said Cornelius. 'What was that all about?'

I told him.

'That does it!' he snapped, in his crisp, military manner, 'I'll get you protection. If I have to twist the arm of every general in the building, I'll get you protection!'

CHAPTER 17

It was the fire that made me see red. It was the straw that broke the back of this little camel's patience. Time was slipping by, the shadows were creeping up the sundial, a young girl was dead, my loved ones were threatened, my home was attacked. I was angry now, angry as an Arabian bull ant, and nothing would stop me.

After Rachel and I, with the help of a few neighbours, had cleaned up the worst of the mess, I rang a friend in the building trade, and arranged for the front of our home and office to be cleaned and painted.

By the time this was done, Cornelius' 'help' had arrived: a hairy ape of a soldier who said, 'Someone give you trouble — I break his arm. Both arms. And maybe a leg.' Then he took up his sentry post at the front door.

Reassuring Momma that she was protected now, I grabbed Rachel by the hand and almost dragged her out the door.

We hailed a passing cab — a wide-bodied, two-horse-powered chariot. 'East Circular Road, cabbie,' I shouted as we leaped aboard, 'and step on it.'

The One Temple was on the outskirts of Caesarea, in the foothills on the eastern edge of the city. Our cab carried us through a residential area of luxury villas, and dropped us on a deserted street beyond the last of the houses. As the rattle of the departing cab faded, a silence settled, broken only by the faint cry of a distant crow and the rustle of the wind through the grapevines that climbed the hill behind the temple.

It was a square building, brightly painted with oriental designs. I tried the front door. It appeared to be locked. That was when I noticed the sign hanging beside the door. It read:

Silent Meditation
In Progress
Visitors Not Admitted
So Sorry

'So what do we do now?' asked Rachel.

'We have no choice. We come back later.'

There was not a cab to be seen on that dusty road, but we managed to hitch a ride with a passing farm wagon back to the centre of the city. From there we walked through the narrow lanes of the financial district, and out onto the coast road.

This took us to the northern sandhills where The Inner Temple, the next on Abi's list, had been erected. With its tinted glass and gilded columns, it looked more like an expensive restaurant than a temple.

The front doors slid open automatically as we approached, and we found ourselves in a plush, carpeted lobby, dotted with potted palms and soft furniture. Quiet music drifted out of hidden speakers.

On the far side of this vast lobby was a reception desk.

'Good morning and welcome to The Inner Temple.' The blonde-haired receptionist smiled as we approached, her teeth like gleaming tombstones. 'Is this your first visit?'

'Yes, and…' I began.

'In that case, I'll just ask you to fill out these membership forms, I'll take down a few particulars, and then you can pay your joining fee either by cash, cheque or credit card.'

'Hang on, sister,' said Rachel, 'we're here to investigate this dump, not join it!'

The receptionist looked shocked. So, frankly, did I. But it got results.

'Oh. Well, perhaps you'd better speak to our Marketing Manager. I'll fetch him for you. Won't be a moment. Just take a seat.'

With that she hurried off, her brow wrinkled with worry.

While we were waiting, a group of people entered through double doors on one side of the lobby and made their way to the front entrance. At the centre of the group was a striking-looking woman: a mass of wild red hair, large green eyes, and a highly mobile mouth (emphasised by a slash of scarlet lipstick) identified her at once as Hortensia Ignorantias. Hortensia was the fashionable guru among the smart set, and the star attraction at The Inner Temple.

Surrounding her was a crowd of simpering sycophants, men and women whose clothes suggested more money than sense, and whose jewellery jangled as they hovered around the popular pundit.

'Oh, Hortensia, your talk today was just woooonderful!' they gushed, as she autographed copies of her latest scroll.

Hortensia saw the mob out of the front door, and then marched back briskly the way she had come.

I was about comment to Rachel about the Hortensia phenomenon when I noticed that we were being approached by a distinguished-looking middle-aged gentleman accompanied by the receptionist with the flashing teeth.

'Good morning, I am Lord Weekly, the Marketing Manager of The Inner Temple,' he said.

He had slicked-down silver hair, a smarmy smile, and a large cigar clenched between his teeth. He spoke with an odd accent that I recognised as belonging to the savage natives of the islands of Britannia.

'*Lord* Weekly?' asked Rachel.

'Yes indeed, my dear. Back in my home town of Londinium I am a member of the nobility. Now, what exactly can I do for you?'

'We have been hired to investigate a murder, Lord Weekly.'

'A murder! Goodness gracious me! We have nothing to do with murders here at The Inner Temple. No, never, nothing of that sort. Not here.'

'The victim,' I explained, 'was a young woman named Abigail Jacobson. Most of her time in the weeks before her death was occupied in visiting a variety of temples. Including this one. Do you remember her?'

'A lot of people come here. Can I be expected to remember every one of them? We're very popular, you know. Oh yes, very popular indeed. A nice little earner this place is at the moment, a nice little earner indeed.'

'I have a photograph here of Abigail,' said Rachel, 'if that would help you remember.'

'Of course, if she did come here,' said Lord Weekly, ignoring Rachel's remark, and ignoring the photograph, 'we would have a record of it. I could check our records if you like.'

'Yes, I would like,' I said. 'How about you do that.'

'Certainly, certainly. Anything to oblige the forces of law and order. Why don't you wait in the piano bar while I check the files? Just step this way.'

And without giving us a moment either to agree or to resist, Lord Weekly led us through the side double doors and up a flight of stairs into what he called the piano bar. This turned out to be...well...a piano bar.

You know the sort of thing: thick pile carpet, dim lighting, a bar along one wall staffed by handsome young men in dark-coloured uniforms, and someone tickling the ivories of a baby grand at the far end of the room.

Lord Weekly left us, hurrying away muttering the word 'files' under his breath.

'I must admit,' said Rachel, 'that I never expected to find a piano bar in a temple.'

I could only nod in surprised agreement.

The long wall opposite the bar was floor-to-ceiling tinted glass. Walking over to it I discovered that we were on a mezzanine floor overlooking a large gymnasium-like hall. In the hall were perhaps three dozen people, all wearing tracksuits, all squatting in the lotus position, and all concentrating on what an attractive young woman at the front of the hall was saying to them.

'Would you like to hear what's going on?' asked the barman from over my shoulder. 'I can turn up the speaker, if you like.'

'Sure,' I replied, 'I'm intrigued.'

He adjusted a knob and the sound from the hall came tinkling out of small speakers overhead. The first thing we heard was the low thump of rhythmical music, and then over the top of the music came the voice of the young woman leading the group.

'Come on now,' she was saying, 'picture a beach, a beautiful beach, it's a beach you've always wanted to visit. Work on it, work on it, see those waves, and see those palm trees. Raise your right arm and you can feel the gentle tropical breeze.'

At this command right arms all over the gym shot up into the air and began to wave about.

'Feel that breeze,' commanded the young woman. 'It's a warm tropical breeze. Now reach down to your feet and pick up a handful of sand. Let that sand trickle through your fingers.'

They all faithfully mimed sand trickling through fingers.

'It's soft warm sand. And it's making you feel very soft and warm too.'

The faces in the gym took on beatific — if not entirely convincing — smiles.

I walked across to the bar and ordered a couple of drinks — a scotch and soda for me (those savage Celts sure know what do with malt) and a Tiberian tonic water for Rachel.

'Tell me,' I said to the barman as I paid for our drinks, 'what exactly is that?'

'They're meditating,' he replied.

'Meditating?'

'It's a form of meditation invented by Hortensia. She calls it "inner fitness" or "soul-ercize." It's very popular with the members here.'

'Oh. I see,' I said. (Well, what else could you say?)

At this point Lord Weekly came bustling into the piano bar carrying a sheet of paper.

'She has been here, I can confirm that,' he said. 'This is the membership form she filled in the day she arrived.'

'And when was that?'

'Unfortunately, the date is a little smudged.'

I held out my hand for the form, but he seemed reluctant to part with it.

'I shouldn't really give you this, you know,' he said. 'Confidential information, you understand.'

'Confidential, my eye! Abigail is dead — her murderer must be found. Nothing is confidential in a murder investigation.'

'Well, if you put it like that...'

And he handed over the slip of paper. I glanced at it quickly. He was right, the date was smudged, and that was pity. Still, a close examination later on might reveal something useful. I folded the form and slipped it into my toga.

Chapter 18

'And what did Abigail do while she was here?'

'Well,' said Lord Weekly, a little reluctantly, 'her membership card shows she tried a little of everything.'

Rachel and I glanced at each other: this was typical of Abigail's behaviour.

'So what did this smorgasbord consist of?'

'Smorgasbord? Oh, yes, I see what you mean! Very good, sir. Very well put indeed.'

'What did Abigail do here?' I insisted.

'Well, she attended one those sessions,' said Weekly, gesturing with his cigar at the 'soul-ercize' going on in the gym. 'She came to a motivational talk, and she attended one of Hortensia's seminars. A bit of everything, as I say. According to her membership card.'

'Did she try to find out the beliefs of the temple?'

'I believe she did talk to one of our counsellors, yes.'

'And what did this counsellor tell her?'

'Ah well, there you're taking me off my territory. I am, you will understand, merely the Marketing Manager. Why don't I track down the counsellor concerned, and you can put your questions directly — how would that be?'

'That would be fine,' I replied.

'Let me see now. According to her card the session

was with Julius Mentor. Come with me, and we will see if he is in his office.'

We had to walk briskly to keep up with Lord Weekly as he led us out of the piano bar, through another set of doors, and down a broad corridor.

The corridor continued the theme of luxury: thick, plush pile carpet, and light timber-panelled walls decorated with original paintings. A series of doors opened off this corridor at regular intervals. Lord Weekly stopped at one of these doors and flung it open.

'Mentor,' he turned to us as if to introduce us, and suddenly realised that he didn't even know our names, 'I'm terribly sorry for my ill manners. You are...?'

'Ben and Rachel Bartholomew. If we can just have a few minutes of your time, Mr Mentor.'

'Of course, take a seat.'

'I'll leave you people to it then,' said Weekly, 'I hope the investigation goes well. Cheery bye.'

And with that he disappeared rapidly out the door, and closed it behind him.

'We are investigating the movements of a young woman who was murdered recently. Her name is Abigail Jacobson, and according to Lord Weekly's record card she spoke to you when she visited this temple.'

'Abigail Jacobson?'

'Here's her photograph,' offered Rachel.

'Ah, yes. I remember her. A most attractive young woman. Murder, you say? How awful.'

'Tragic. Describe her frame of mind when she spoke to you.'

'Very open-minded. Full of questions. Definitely

someone in search of satisfaction, in search of…well…'

'Truth?'

'Yes, that's probably the best word.'

'And were you able to help her in her search?'

'One hopes so. One can only do one's humble best.'

'And exactly what is "one's" humble best? What did you tell her? What, precisely, did she want to know?'

'She asked about the beliefs of the temple, and the teachings of Hortensia — that sort of thing.'

'Well, tell us,' I persisted. 'Tell us what you told her.'

'Very well then. Hortensia teaches that the self is the prime reality. That's the first and most important thing. The second thing is that the self is surrounded by a dual universe: there's the visible universe (accessible to consciousness) and the invisible universe (accessible to altered consciousness). You with me so far?'

'Haven't missed a beat — keep going.'

'Well, in altered consciousness, which Hortensia calls cosmic consciousness, space, time and morality disappear.'

'How convenient,' muttered Rachel.

'What was that?' asked Mentor.

'Never mind, keep going.'

'Very well then. Hortensia also teaches that the self does not end at death — which is just a transition to another form.'

'Reincarnation, in other words?'

'Precisely. Hortensia, for example, can remember many of her previous lives. She has written about them in her best-selling scrolls. And under hypnosis many of our members here are able to recall past lives. And very interesting those past lives often are too.'

'That's what I've noticed,' said Rachel sardonically.

'Pardon?' said Mentor.

'Why is it that everyone who recalls a past life recalls being a princess, an emperor, a pharaoh, or a maharaja? Why does no one ever recall a past life as a slave in a salt mine? Or as the sweeper in the camel stables? Or as a leper? You don't have many lepers turn up in these "past life" recall sessions, do you?'

'I can't actually remember any, no,' admitted Mentor.

'Tell me something. This universe experienced by altered, or cosmic, consciousness — just what is it?' I asked.

'Ah, well. On that point there is some disagreement.'

'Explain, please.'

'There are three views. Some say the universe experienced by altered consciousness is separate from the self — this is the occult view. Some say it is a projection of the self — this is the psychedelic view. And some say that everything is a private experience within the self and has no objective truth whatsoever.'

'A little confusing.'

'Mind you, Hortensia favours the first of those views, and that tends to prevail at this temple.'

'Well thank you for your time, Mr Mentor,' I said rising to my feet.

'I'll take you down to Lord Weekly's office, and

he will offer you any further help you may need,' said Mentor, opening the door.

Mentor led us down the plush corridor, and past several doors. He stopped at one, and, without waiting for a reply, opened it as he knocked.

This office repeated the theme of plush luxury — thick pile carpet, vast oak desk, original paintings on the walls. A large window overlooked the 'spiritual gym' in which the 'soul-ercise' was still going on.

Well-equipped though the office was, it lacked just one thing — namely, Lord Weekly himself.

'Funny. I was sure he'd be here,' said Mentor.

Just then the connecting door to the next office swung open and Lord Weekly entered. Through the open doorway we glimpsed a room that looked to be only half the size of Weekly's office, and lined with heavy, dark curtains.

'I've just been in my private meditation room,' explained Weekly, and he sat down behind his desk. 'Thank you for looking after our visitors, Mentor, I will take over now.'

Mentor accepted this as his dismissal and left the office.

'Have all your questions been answered now?' asked Lord Weekly, with a smarmy smile.

'You and your staff have been most helpful,' replied Rachel, matching his dripping saccharin sweetness-for-sweetness, although I doubt that Weekly detected the irony in Rachel's voice.

'We aim to please, my dear. Never hesitate to contact us at any time.'

As he said these words Lord Weekly was rising from his desk, clearly about to usher us out, but was interrupted when the door burst open and Hortensia Ignorantias herself swept into the room.

'Arthur, about my seminar tonight...' she began.

Then she spotted us and stopped, her eyes narrowed, and she took on the look of a rat-catcher spotting two fat and particularly juicy rats.

'Hello, my dears,' she said, 'I don't believe we've met.'

'Hortensia, my love,' said Weekly, 'these are the two detectives who are investigating the tragic...er...murder...of that young woman I told you about.'

'Ah yes! Of course!' exclaimed Hortensia, 'I can see the aura of darkness and tragedy that hangs around you. You poor dears. You should come to my seminar tonight. If the spirit of Tantalus makes contact (as I am sure he will) you will find great comfort in his wisdom. Everyone does.'

There was something powerful and larger than life about Hortensia: from the bold slash of scarlet lipstick that made her mouth seem even larger and more mobile than it was, the many layers of swirling silk in which she dressed, the silver earrings that flashed in the light, to the necklace of extraordinarily large pearls that encircled her white throat — it all added up to a walking, human neon sign saying 'pay attention!'. And people did.

'Why don't you do that?' said Weekly, who seemed, for some reason, to want to hurry us out of the office. 'Come back tonight. Come to the seminar. You'll be most impressed by the appearance of Tantalus — everyone is.'

'Nice to have met you, Miss Ignorantias,' I managed to get out, before we were hustled out the door. Then I realised that we hadn't actually met her; at least we hadn't been introduced.

Back in the lobby downstairs Lord Weekly kept babbling as he led us to the front door.

'It is, as dear Hortensia says, a most tragic business. Very tragic, very sad indeed. A young woman cut off in the prime of life like that. Hortensia is very sensitive you know, oh yes, very sensitive indeed. A young woman full of life one day, found in a ditch the next, Hortensia feels that sort of thing. You really should come to one of her seminars.'

At the front door he left us, and as we walked out I could hear him saying to the receptionist behind our backs, 'Nothing to worry about there. Just a storm in a goblet, that's all. It'll blow over.'

'Well,' said Rachel, as we stood on the street, in the blazing heat of the sun, 'that has to be the oddest of the lot!'

CHAPTER 19

Back home in our apartment I telephoned Cornelius to report on The Inner Temple.

I told him it was another disappointment: more people wrapped up in a philosophy that was all about themselves. He asked about the occult aspects of the temple, and whether there was any danger there. I explained that there are only two explanations of the occult. One is delusion, either self-delusion or clever trickery. The other is that the spirit realm they are tapping into is real, but that it's controlling them, not the other way around.

Later, over lunch, I noticed that Rachel was merely playing with the salad Momma had served up.

'Something on your mind?' I asked.

'I was thinking about Hortensia,' she replied. 'She certainly knows how to lay it on with a trowel...'

'And a shovel and a wheelbarrow!' I added. 'By the way, I'm still puzzled by this mysterious Haunted Temple no one seems to know anything about. So I thought I'd advertise.'

'Advertise?'

'Yeah. A small ad in the classifieds.'

'Saying what?'

'Something along the lines of: "Have you heard of The Haunted Temple? All information supplied will be treated confidentially and generously rewarded." And then put our postal address.'

'Don't say "generously".'

'Why not?'

'You'll only encourage the fortune-hunters who know nothing, to make up something to sell.'

'You're right. Okay, I'll drop "generously." In fact, to avoid that problem, why don't I drop all reference to a reward? Just say: "All information supplied will be treated confidentially." That way we should only hear from the genuine.'

'That's much better. Run the ad like that.'

As soon as lunch was over I telephoned the offices of the *Acta Diurna* and lodged the ad. I booked it to run for the rest of the week. They assured me that it would appear in tomorrow's edition.

'That's that,' I said to Rachel. 'Now it's time to try The One Temple again.'

It was not long after lunchtime that we found ourselves back in the foothills on the outskirts of town, standing in front of that square building, richly decorated with oriental designs.

I noticed that the most repeated pattern in the design, however, was not oriental at all. It was simply a plain red circle, and it appeared again and again in the decorations that covered the face of the building.

This time there was no notice posted, and the front door swung open at my touch.

There was a tinkle of wind-chimes as Rachel and I entered. In contrast to the bright oriental illustrations on the exterior, the interior was dark and rather plain. Heavy timber panelling was the chief feature; and solid, dark timber pillars created the impression of an indoor forest.

Painted on each of the pillars was the symbol of the temple: the red circle — just like the letter 'O'.

Making our way slowly forward through the gloom

we came to what might be called a 'clearing' in this indoor forest. Seated, cross-legged in a circle in the clearing, were perhaps twenty young men.

They all wore plain, dull brownish robes and had their heads shaved in the oriental fashion. But they were not from the East. Judging by their faces they were Roman, Greek, Egyptian; a few even looked Jewish. Painted on each of their foreheads was the red circle of the temple.

They were humming — a long, low, single note. As we approached, the humming turned into a chant: 'One...one...one...one' they chanted.

The single syllable of their chant was lengthened into a kind of hum: 'One...one...one...one' as they chanted.

I felt my sleeve being tugged and turned around to find a young woman at my elbow. She wore the same dish-water dull brown robe as the men, but her head wasn't shaved — instead, her long black hair was heavily threaded with beads, and small brass rings pierced her ears and her nose.

Under the fringe of her hair I could see the temple's red circle painted on her forehead.

'You must not disturb the men's meditating,' she said in a hushed voice.

'Who's in charge here?' I asked in a whisper.

'Follow me,' was her reply.

When we were far enough removed from the chanting circle the woman said, 'How may I be of assistance to you?'

'I am Ben Bartholomew and this is my wife Rachel,' I explained. 'A young woman has been murdered and we are trying to trace her movements in the time leading up to her death. One of the places she came was here.'

'You must ask the Lama; he will know. The Lama knows all.'

'The Lama?'

'He is our Spiritual Master. His full and proper title is The Brahma Lama with the Calmer Karma. I will take you to him.'

She led the way to the far side of the temple. There was a series of doors leading to side rooms. We were led into one of these.

It turned out to be a sparsely furnished cell: there was a small bowl of water with petals floating in it, one fat candle burning brightly, and one woven rush mat. Seated on the mat was a middle-aged oriental wearing a yellow robe.

The young woman did not introduce us; instead she just bowed and backed out of the room while still crouched in the bowed position.

There was a long silence.

I looked at Rachel and Rachel looked me. I gestured at the floor, and Rachel nodded her head as if to say, 'Might as well.'

We both lowered ourselves into a cross-legged position on the floor where we could look at the Lama eye to eye. Still he ignored us.

I coughed a few times, but got no response.

'Excuse me,' I said at last, 'if we're not interrupting, may we have a moment of your time?'

'My son, my daughter,' he said, inclining his head slightly to look at us directly, 'you seek enlightenment?'

'After a fashion,' said Rachel.

'We are private investigators,' I explained. 'Ben and Rachel Bartholomew. A young woman has been murdered and we are trying to trace her movements in the time leading up to her death.'

'I have a photograph of her here,' said Rachel. 'Perhaps you will recognise it.'

'She was here,' said the Lama, giving the photograph a barely cursory glance. 'She attended my lecture and spoke to me afterwards.'

'What about?'

'She sought True Enlightenment. She wished to be taught the Pathway to Peace.'

'Tell us,' I said, 'tell us what you told her.'

'It may be too simple for you too understand. But perhaps you will be able to stoop towards the truth.'

'Give it a shot.'

'This is the truth: The One is everything, and everything is The One. Why is it then, you will ask, that some people are so unhappy?'

(I've gotta admit, that was not the question that had occurred to me at that point.)

'Including your young friend,' continued the Lama, apparently unable to read my sceptical thoughts, 'She was deeply unhappy.'

'What could you do for her unhappiness?'

'What can the donkey do for the dove? What can the camel do for the fox?'

'I'm afraid I don't follow.'

'You are too occidental — too Western in your thinking,' he explained, 'East is east, and west is west.'

'Yeah. And north is north, and south is south,' I thought to myself. Out loud I asked, 'What does that mean?'

The Lama continued: 'There is a hierarchy — a Great Chain of Being — such that some things, and some people, are more at one with The One than others. I explained to your young friend that all roads lead to The One. I told her that in escaping the illusion of this world and realising The One, what matters is method, not mind.'

He dipped his finger in the waterbowl, traced a wet circle in the dust on the floor, and then continued: 'To realise your oneness with The One is to pass beyond personality.'

Then he traced a second circle. 'To realise your oneness with The One is to pass beyond knowledge.'

Then a third circle. 'To realise your oneness with The One is to pass beyond good and evil.'

There was a long silence, and then the Lama asked, 'Your young friend has died, you said?'

'Yes — murdered.'

'I told her that death is the end of the individual, but it changes nothing.'

'A week ago Abigail was alive, today she is not — that looks to me like a change.'

'Time is unreal,' said the Lama. 'History is cyclical. The present is eternal.'

Seeing as how sitting cross-legged was making my joints ache and my underwear bunch, I was certainly hoping that the present was not eternal.

'A pupil once went to a great Master,' continued the Lama, 'and asked: "Oh Master, how may I know that death changes nothing?" The Master replied: "Sit beneath the branch of the tree that holds the nest of the crow, and listen to what the crow says at midnight." So that pupil sat beneath that branch every night, night after night, season after season. After twelve years he returned to the Master and said: "Oh Master, the crow says nothing at midnight." To which the Master replied: "Now you know that death changes nothing." I know this, for I was that pupil.'

Having delivered himself of this, the Lama closed

his eyes and seemed to drift back into his sub-hyp-
notic state.

Rachel and I looked at each other and raised our
eyebrows as if to say, 'And people pay good money
for this?'

CHAPTER 20

Rachel and I both stretched out our cramped legs and stood up to leave.

As we turned towards the door, from behind us came the voice of the Lama: 'Remember what one of our great poets has said: "The happy rock dreams furiously." '

And before either Rachel or I could respond he added, 'And don't raise your eyebrows at me again!'

We made our way back to the front door of the temple, both trying politely to hide our grins.

'Well,' said Rachel with a sigh, as we stepped out into the bright Mediterranean sunshine, 'What did you get out of that little lot?'

'What is to be got out of an empty pot? What is left in your cup when you have drunk the wine?' I replied.

'Now don't you start! I've had quite enough of that sort of thing!' and she punched me playfully on the arm.

'I got nothing out of it, sweetheart,' I said in my own defence. 'And Abigail, I suspect, got exactly the same, since we know that she went on from here to The Inner Temple.'

'And, apart from the mysterious Haunted Temple we have now got to the end of Abigail's list. So, where does the investigation go from here?'

'Three things to do: check out Abigail's employers,

maybe re-check one or two of the temples, and wait for a response to the newspaper ad — it's vital we get a lead on this Haunted Temple.'

By the time we got back to our apartment the sun was setting over the Mediterranean in brilliant flames of scarlet and gold.

We had been at home only long enough to kick off our sandals, loosen the belts on our robes, and flop into an easy chair when the front door crashed opened and footsteps pounded up the stairs.

Our lounge-room door was flung open and there was Captain Cornelius — flushed in the face and out of breath.

'Ben...Rachel...' he gasped.

'What's happened?' I asked.

'It must have been something terrible!' said Rachel, taking Cornelius gently by one arm and leading him to a chair.

'No...no...' he gasped, still fighting for breath as he sat down, 'wonderful...not terrible.'

'Here, drink this,' said Momma, waddling in with a goblet full of cold water.

Cornelius gulped down the drink like a camel straight from the sands of the Sahara.

'Ben...Rachel...' he said, still puffing, but his breath slowly returning, 'I felt that I must tell someone what has happened...and I thought of you two.'

'I'm glad you thought of us,' said Rachel. 'Now — what has happened?'

Speaking rapidly and breathlessly, Cornelius told us that God had spoken to him. The message, he said, was clear: to understand God's plan for this world, and for his life, Cornelius should send messengers to fetch a man named Peter, who was visiting the city of Joppa, down the coast. 'And I've sent some people, post haste,' he concluded. 'They left less than half an hour ago.'

Captain Cornelius sank back into his chair to catch his breath after telling this story in a rush of words.

Momma looked at me and raised her eyebrows. I knew what she was thinking: God has no dealings with non-Jews — who does this Italian think he is, claiming to have a message from God?

'What do you think?' asked Cornelius.

'It's, ah, remarkable,' I replied, non-committally.

'I think it's…interesting,' said Rachel, quietly and thoughtfully.

Cornelius stayed with us for over an hour, speculating about what would happen when his men reached Peter with the message.

Rachel and I were subdued: we knew what was likely to happen. As well as being a Christian, Peter was a strict Jew, born and bred, and we couldn't picture him having anything to do with a non-Jew who imagined he had messages from God.

Later over dinner, after Cornelius had left, Momma said, 'He's a nice man, but where does he get off thinking God talks to him? We Jews are God's people, God talks to Jews! Italians! What do they know?'

'What do you really think of his "vision," Ben,' asked Rachel.

'To be honest,' I replied, somewhat reluctantly, 'to be really frank…'

'Yes — go on.'

'Well…I wondered if he had a drinking problem.'

'You think he was drunk this afternoon?'

'How else can you explain it?' I responded.

'But he certainly wasn't drunk when he came here,' insisted Rachel.

'No, that's true enough,' I admitted. 'So what do you make of it?'

'I don't know...I really don't know,' she said quietly.

'At any rate, he's headed for a disappointment,' I said sadly. 'I can't imagine Peter responding to his message.'

'I suppose you're right,' said Rachel slowly. 'But perhaps...'

'Perhaps what?'

'Oh...nothing...'

I knew from experience that when Rachel was in that sort of mood, nothing could extract her thoughts from her, so I let it go.

The next morning Dr Nostrum rang from the morgue to ask us if we would like to pick up Abigail's personal effects and return them to her parents. I said we would.

Our hearts were heavy as we approached the Jacobson house carrying the canvas bag that Dr Nostrum had given us containing Abigail's clothes and her pitifully few personal possessions.

I had telephoned ahead to warn them we were coming, and Joe was waiting for us. He opened the front door personally, at my first knock, and ushered us into the atrium of their villa, where Hannah was waiting.

'How are you two coping now?' asked Rachel, as she slipped an arm around Hannah's shoulders.

Joe shrugged and said, 'We'll survive. Somehow. We have to. Life goes on.'

'But it will never be the same,' said Hannah.

'Here are the things,' I said quietly, handing the bag to Joe. Hannah, however, had heard.

'Let me see,' she said.

'It will only upset you,' said Joe, 'you know that.'

'Please,' insisted Hannah, 'I want to.'

'Very well,' said Joe, with a shrug of his shoulders.

Very gently, as though she were handling a child, Hannah opened up the canvas bag and shook the contents onto a marble-topped table that stood in the middle of the atrium.

Moving slowly, like a person in a dream, she began to smooth out the clothes, and then fold them neatly.

'Are you alright, Hannah?' asked Joe, looking worried.

'Yes, I'm fine,' she replied, in a quiet, distant voice.

Then Hannah began to separate the clothing from the other items: clothes in one pile; next to that, shoes and the leather belt from Abigail's toga; and next to that, a few modest items of jewellery — just some bangles and a thin silver chain she had worn around her neck.

'Is anything missing?' I asked, as gently as I could.

'Her purse is missing,' said Joe. 'She always carried a small leather purse in her pocket.'

'And what was in the purse?' I asked. 'Were the contents valuable?'

'She carried a little money, that's all. Just a denarius or two. Never much.'

'So, the purse and money are missing,' I continued. 'Anything else?'

'Her little pieces of paper,' replied Hannah, her eyes becoming misty and a sob entering her voice.

'I beg your pardon?'

'Pieces of paper. She had a habit, you see, of writing herself notes on little scraps of papyrus and stuffing them into her pockets. There are none here.'

'The murderer seems to have emptied out the pockets completely,' I whispered to Rachel.

'Exactly,' Rachel whispered back. 'But why?'

'Why' was just the question I couldn't answer at that point.

'And her handkerchief is missing,' continued Hannah, apparently not having noticed our exchange.

'And...her earrings are gone!' she said in a louder voice, with a touch of anger in it.

'Her earrings?' asked Rachel.

'They were silver earrings. Large dangling ones. Star-shaped. They used to catch the light, and flash and sparkle, as she turned her head. They're missing.'

Hannah appeared to be more upset by the missing earrings than anything else.

'Were they valuable?' I asked.

'They were the most valuable things she owned,' replied Joe. 'So that's why she was killed! For her earrings!'

'Perhaps,' I said. 'Can you give me an exact description of them. Perhaps draw me a sketch?'

'Sure. But what good will it do?'

'Whoever stole them will want to dispose of them to a fence — to turn them into cash. I can get Cornelius to circulate a description to all the officers of the city watch — and that might give us a lead on the killer.'

'I see. Just give me a second. I'll grab a piece of parchment and do you a drawing.'

While Joe was doing this Hannah was sitting hunched over the marble table-top, fingering Abigail's possessions.

'And something else is missing,' she said, after a long silence, and added quietly 'My Abigail is missing.'

Then she buried her face in her hands and sobbed loudly.

CHAPTER 21

Herod's palace was the sort of building you would expect from a man with more money than taste. In fact, Herod the Great was a man noted for having more money than a Greek shipping magnate — and no one ever noticed him having any taste at all.

Apparently he had called in a Roman architect and said: 'Build me a palace — and make it look like a palace.' And that's what he got.

Now, years after his death, Herod's palace was the home of the Roman Governor of the Province of Judea, a former soldier named Pontius Pilate. I had had some dealings with Pilate in the past, and on that occasion I discovered that his vanity had swollen up and occupied the place where his brain used to be.

This time, however, it wasn't Pilate I was coming to see.

Rachel and I entered the marbled entrance lobby as big as a gladiators' arena and approached the reception desk.

'May I help you, sir? Madam?' asked the young woman behind the desk in the bored inflections of a public servant who would be happy to never serve the public.

'Sorry to interrupt your reading,' I said, looking at the glossy magazines covering her desk.

'Just tell me what you want.'

'We would like to see Mr Mediocritas, please.'

'Do you have an appointment?'

'I'm afraid not.'

'In that case he won't see you.'

'Ask.'

'There's no point. I'm telling you — he won't see you.'

'Try.'

'If you insist. But it's a waste of time.'

She picked up her telephone and dialled an internal number.

'Tell him,' I said, 'it's about a murder.'

We all waited while the phone rang at the other end. Then a loud click told us it had been picked up.

'I'm sorry to disturb you, Mr Mediocritas, sir. It's front desk reception here. There's a man and woman out here who want to see you, sir. No sir, they don't have an appointment. I told them that, sir. They said to tell you it's about a murder, sir. I'll ask them, sir. He says: what murder?'

'The murder of one of his staff.'

'They say the murder of one of you staff, sir. Very well, sir. Thank you, sir,' she put down the phone. 'He said take a seat, someone will come and take you up.'

'Thanks — you've been terrific.'

Rachel and I sat down on one of the marble forms that lined the walls of the entrance lobby and waited.

And waited.

And waited.

'What's taking him so long?' asked Rachel, stifling a yawn.

'He's just proving how important he is by keeping us waiting,' I said.

'It's worse than being at the dentist's. There's not even anything to read while we're waiting.'

At last, a weedy-looking young man with spectacles and no chin shuffled up to where we were sitting.

'You the people waiting to see Mr Mediocritas?' he whined in a voice full of adenoids.

'That's us,' said Rachel.

'Follow me then.'

We rose to our feet, stretched our cramped muscles, and followed him.

He led us up two flights of stairs, passed a second reception desk, and went through a large general office full of scribes busily scratching way with quills on parchment, and into a smaller, more opulent waiting-room.

'Wait here,' said the chinless wonder, and then disappeared before we could ask him any questions.

'Isn't this terrific?' said Rachel sourly. 'We get to wait some more!'

After waiting long enough for the battle of Troy to be fought all over again — complete with slow-motion replays — a door on the far side of the waiting-room opened and figure glided in.

He was a magnificent figure of portly dimensions: he must have had a great barrel chest — until it fell to about the level of his stomach! His Roman nose (which showed signs of having enjoyed too many late night glasses of port) was elevated at a lofty and snobbish angle. Beneath a large mouth were enough rolling chins to cure the chinless wonder and a dozen of his similarly afflicted friends.

'I am Didius Mediocritas. You wished to see me?'

'Yes, my name is Ben Bartholomew and this is...'

'Follow me,' he interrupted, and then turned around and glided out of the room again, moving like a stately ocean liner, without any apparent effort or motion.

Rachel and I followed him into his sprawling private office.

By the time we had waded through carpet as deep as the cattle grasses on the African savannah and found ourselves two seats, Mediocritas was enthroned behind his desk.

This desk in itself was worth noting. It was made entirely from the best-quality Lebanon cedar and was big enough to sleep an average family in the slums of Cairo. Perhaps two families.

'I am Didius Mediocritas. I am the Under Assistant Secretary for State Affairs to the Assistant Secretary of State. What do you wish to speak to me about?'

'You employed a young woman named Abigail Jacobson,' I said, clearing my throat, 'I think she worked in your office.'

'There are many minions working in my office. Many, many minions. And, yes, she was one. And I understand that she is now missing. Her father came to the office making enquiries.'

'Not missing,' said Rachel. 'Dead.'

His right eyebrow went up about half a millimetre.

'Murdered,' I added.

It went up another half a millimetre.

'Distressing news, no doubt. You will pass on my condolences to her family, of course.'

It was a command, not a request.

'Of course. Now, can I ask you...'

'And I will have to advertise her position,' interrupted Mediocritas. 'It is so hard to get good staff these days.'

'Can you tell us something about the young woman, Mr Mediocritas?'

'What would you like to know?'

'What was she like, for a start.'

'Studious. Sensible. Reliable. Not like most young-sters these days.'

'Did she have special friends in the office?'

'I am told not. I have made enquiries, and I am told by my staff that she was quiet, shy, reserved. She got on with her work and made no close friends. She suited my office admirably.'

'If she made no friends, did she make any ene-mies?'

'You don't understand. Now listen carefully, I will explain this only once. She did not produce any reaction in the people around her at all. They did not like her, they did not dislike her. She was quiet, she was shy, she kept to herself.'

'No office romances?' asked Rachel.

'The only young person close to her age is the young man who brought you here.'

He was referring to the bespectacled chinless wonder with the adenoid problem.

'I guess not then,' I said.

'Oh, I don't know,' said Rachel, 'A lonely young girl...well...stranger things have happened.'

'Not here they haven't,' said Mediocritas firmly. 'There were no office romances, I can solemnly assure you of that.'

'Can you think of any reason why anyone would want to murder Abigail?'

'Sir, madam — let me make it abundantly clear that I can think of no reason whatsoever. None, that is, that has any connection with my office. And of what her life consisted outside the office I have not the faintest idea.'

'So you can think of no...'

'I have no intention of repeating myself. I have said what I said once, and that should be enough for anyone except a nincompoop. I have no intention of sitting here repeating myself all afternoon. You may leave the same way you came in.'

With that, he turned his attention to reading a large report that was sitting on his desk. The interview, it appeared, was over.

CHAPTER 22

Rachel and I had risen to our feet and turned towards the exit when a double door on the opposite side of the room burst open and a party of people entered.

At the centre of the group was a remarkable couple. She was tall, green-eyed, with a mass of tinted, curled hair; he was short and swarthy, wearing a military uniform with so many medals across his chest it was a miracle he remained upright.

I had come across these two once before: they were the Governor of the Province of Judea, Pontius Pilate, and his wife, the Lady Claudia.

Pilate began talking the moment the door opened in a non-stop babble of words: 'Ihavebeen-workingtoohard...'

Mediocritas pushed his bulky frame to his feet and adopted a posture that roughly resembled standing to attention.

'...muchtoohard,' continued Pilate, 'Ineedabreak.'

'Yes sir,' murmured the man who was the Under Assistant Secretary for State Affairs to the Assistant Secretary of State.

'Whoarethesetwo?'

'These...ah...persons, are...ah...detectives, sir.'

That made Pilate draw a deep breath and talk a little slower. 'Detectives?' he queried, his eyebrows climbing up his forehead like two hairy beetles in a race to the bald spot, 'Whadda we need detectives around here for?'

'One of my staff members (a very junior staff member, I assure you sir) has been murdered.'

'Very careless of you, Mediocritas, to hire people who get themselves murdered. Very careless indeed.'

'I'll see that it doesn't happen again, sir.'

'You do that.'

Pilate was now squinting hard in my direction.

'I've met you somewhere before, haven't I?' he asked.

'Yes, I was...' I began.

'Don't tell me! Don't tell me! Let me remember. I've been training my memory lately. I hired this Greek guy as my memory trainer. Hang on, it'll come back to me in a moment.'

Everyone in the room stood in frozen silence while His Excellency wrinkled his brow in a mighty effort to remember.

The silence weighed more and more heavily, until at length I felt as though one of Hannibal's elephants was leaning against me, weary from a long day's march and trying to catch its breath.

I opened my mouth to speak.

'Don't tell me!' snapped Pilate, before I could utter a sound.

'You were in Jerusalem, weren't you?' asked the Governor, while Lady Claudia examined her fingernails and looked bored.

'Yes sir, I...'

'That's it — Jerusalem! I knew I'd remember! You were an officer in the city watch — that's right, isn't it?'

'Well, actually...' I began.

'Yes, yes, of course. An officer in the city watch.

You arrested that terrorist guy…you know, what's his name?'

'Barabbas, sir,' offered Mediocritas.

'That's what I was about to say! Don't interrupt me when I'm remembering. You arrested that terrorist guy Barabbas. That was a good piece of work, Mr…Mr…'

'Bartholomew, sir, but I…'

'I know! I know! No need to prompt me! It was a good piece of work, Mr Bartholomew.'

'Actually I…'

'Oh, don't be modest about it. You did very well on that occasion. It's just unfortunate that we had to let the guy go. Some dumb custom about the whatsit festival.'

'Passover Festival,' said Mediocritas, unwisely.

'I warned you!' yelled Pilate and he whirled around angrily to face his Under Assistant Secretary for the etc. etc. 'Just for that — you're not coming on our outing tomorrow.'

'Outing, sir?' muttered a miserable Mediocritas.

'Yes, outing. That's what I came to tell you. I want a Roman galley with a full complement of slaves ready after breakfast tomorrow. And make those slaves the fittest, strongest rowers you can find — I want to go waterskiing.'

'Yes, sir.'

'As for you…' continued Pilate, turning back to me, '…Mr…ah…Mr Barabbas, keep up the good work detecting.'

He turned on his heels and stomped out of the office. Perhaps returning to his Greek trainer for another memory lesson.

Left behind, Lady Claudia drifted over to where Rachel and I stood.

'You two,' she murmured in a soft, languid voice.

'Yes, ma'am?'

'You two have such a dark aura around you.'

'Dark aura, ma'am?' said Rachel.

'I can see it hovering above your heads. A sort of dark purple colour it is.'

'You must understand,' said Mediocritas firmly, making a diplomatic intervention, and looking squarely at Rachel and me, 'you must understand that Her Excellency has clairvoyant gifts. She is Very Sensitive to such things.'

'Thank you, Mediocritas! There's no need to explain everything!' said Lady Claudia sharply. (Poor Mediocritas, his every effort to help was being squashed unceremoniously.)

'I see Fields,' continued Lady Claudia.

'Fields of flowers?' I asked tentatively, thinking that she might be switching from clairvoyance to poetry.

'Fields of Power! Idiot! I don't know why I waste my time with you people!'

'I apologise for my husband,' said Rachel in her most gracious voice. 'Do go on Lady Claudia.'

'Clearly you are a Sensitive yourself, my child,' replied Her Excellency, looking pleased.

Rachel somehow managed to blush nicely on cue, and lower her eyelids demurely. This was the most un-Rachel-like performance I'd ever seen.

'I will explain...for the benefit of the girl here. She, at least, appears to be interested. I can see auras, Fields of Power, surrounding people. And the aura surrounding you two is the deepest shade of purple I have ever seen in an aura. Actually, it's quite a nice shade of purple — I had a robe that colour once. When I was young.'

Lady Claudia wasn't just off the with auras, she was off with the pixies!

'And what does a purple aura mean, your Ladyship?' asked Rachel politely.

'Sadness. Deep, deep sadness. That's what my medium in Rome use, to say. Mind you, Hortensia says it means something quite different.'

'Hortensia?'

'Hortensia Ignorantias of The Inner Temple. Have you heard of her?'

'Yes, your Ladyship, we have heard of her,' replied Rachel. 'Are you a patron of Hortensia Ignorantias?'

'Oh, yes indeed! Very much so. She has seen things in me that my medium in Rome never saw. Mind you, he was only a very medium medium. Quite a common medium, in fact.'

'Not what you'd call a medium rare?' I couldn't stop myself from saying it (and got Rachel's toe sharply in shin for my trouble).

'A what?' asked Lady Claudia, blinking rapidly and staring at me vacantly.

'Nothing, your Ladyship. You were saying?'

'What was I saying? Ah, yes. Hortensia sees *depths* in me, she see *potentials* in me that no one has ever seen before.'

'That must be most encouraging,' murmured Rachel.

'How perceptive of you, child! That's exactly what Hortensia is! She is *so* encouraging!'

'The murdered girl also visited The Inner Temple,' explained Rachel.

'Did she indeed?' said Lady Claudia, sounding suddenly bored by the turn the conversation had taken — after all, it was no longer about her.

'Yes,' persisted Rachel. 'Perhaps you saw her there?'

'Oh, I doubt that, my child.'

'Her name was Abigail Jacobson.'

'Abigail Jacobson? That's a very Jewish-sounding name, isn't it?'

'She was Jewish, your Ladyship.'

'I'm sure I've never heard that name before.'

'Perhaps you'd recognise her picture. This is a photograph of the murdered girl.'

As she spoke Rachel handed over the snapshot of Abigail.

'She is quite a pretty little thing, isn't she?' murmured Lady Claudia.

'"Was," not "is" — she's dead,' insisted Rachel.

'If you say so. It is quite a pretty face, all the same. In a very common sort of way, of course.'

'Have you ever seen her before?'

'Never. Never before.' And as she returned the snapshot Lady Claudia added, 'It is such a deep purple. Your aura, that is. I have never seen an aura so purple before. And Hortensia says that purple doesn't stand for sadness after all.'

'What does she say it stands for?'

'Purple is for peril, she says — it stands for the danger of death!'

And with a swish of her rich robes Lady Claudia spun around and stalked out of the room.

With both of Their Excellencies departed, Mediocritas wiped his brow with a large, white handkerchief. Clearly he found these audiences with Roman governors, and governors' wives, rather trying.

'You two can go now,' he snapped, reaching over

and picking up a small brass bell from his desk, which he rang vigorously.

In a moment the weedy young man with the undersupply of chin and the oversupply of adenoids appeared.

'Show these two out,' said Mediocritas. 'And make sure they leave the building.'

As we marched down the corridors and staircases, back towards the main entrance, Rachel whispered, 'What have we ever done to him?'

'Nothing,' I replied. 'But Pilate and wife gave him a hard time, so he passed it on to us. By the way, what game were you playing in there? Kidding up to the Lady Claudia like that?'

'Well, my dear, undiplomatic husband — you seemed to be going out of your way to offend everyone in power, and that did not strike me as a useful way to go.'

'So you decided to massage a powerful ego?'

'Precisely.'

'But we didn't learn anything of value, did we?'

'True. But we didn't get into hot water either, did we?'

'Also true. Well done, my love — I'm glad you're on the case with me.'

CHAPTER 23

'So, where to next?' asked Rachel, when we were back out on the street.

'Abigail's previous employers,' I replied. 'Perhaps Abigail's death relates to some previous interest in her life — before the fascination with temples, that is.'

'Where do we start?'

'With the tax accountants — the firm of Cursus & Minimis.'

We found them on the very top floor of an old wooden building in one of the narrow lanes behind the Forum. There was no lift, only a flight of rickety stairs, and by the time we got to the top we were almost choking on dust and dry rot.

In the front room of the Cursus & Minimis offices sat a very bored young woman laboriously copying Latin documents by hand.

Above her head was a large, impressively lettered sign, also in Latin: *Tibi gratias agimus quod nihil fumas.*

While we waited for the young woman to finish her work and ask us what we wanted, Rachel turned to me and whispered, 'What does the sign say?'

'It's just a message for the clients.'

'An important legal message?'

'I suppose you could call it that.'

By this time we had been standing in front of the

young woman for a minute or more, but she appeared to be taking great care not to notice us.

'Excuse me,' I said.

The woman looked up at us with a bored expression on her face.

'We'd like to see one of the partners.'

'Wait here, I'll see if someone's available. Who shall I say is calling?'

'Ben and Rachel Bartholomew — private detectives.'

'Oh, I see!' she said, suddenly a little less bored. 'I'll tell them at once then.'

We were left standing in the outer office cooling our heels (an easy thing to do when you're wearing sandals).

'Ben — now we're alone, tell me what that sign means.'

'That big impressive sign on the wall?'

'Yes, that one.'

'That one that says *Tibi gratias agimus quod nihil fumas*?'

'Yes, that one.'

'It means: "Thank you for not smoking." '

At that moment the inner office door opened, the young woman stood to one side holding the door back, and said, 'You can go in now.'

We found ourselves in an office that would have made a broom closet claustrophobic. Its sole occupant was a prematurely bald young man with a permanently worried expression on his face.

'Good morning, I'm Ben Bartholomew, and this is my wife Rachel.'

'How do you do. My name is Subservius. I am the senior clerk. May I help you in some way?'

'We'd rather see one of the partners.'

'That's not possible, I'm afraid. They've hung the *Noli Peturbare* sign on the door, so I can't even tell them you're here.'

'The what sign?' asked Rachel.

'*Noli Peturbare* — Do Not Disturb,' I translated.

'Sorry,' said Subservius in a whining voice, 'but it's more than my job's worth to disturb them when that sign is hanging on their doorknob.'

'Perhaps you could answer some questions for us then?' I suggested.

'I do know they have a very heavy job on just at the moment,' muttered Subservius, who appeared not to have heard my question.

As he spoke he looked over his shoulder at the double doors just behind him. From the brass knob of one of the doors the *Noli Peturbare* sign was dangling at an odd angle.

'A very big job indeed,' he continued. 'They're doing the tax accounts for Archimedes Colossus.'

'Who?' asked Rachel.

'You haven't heard of Archimedes Colossus? The big Greek inventor?'

'What did he invent?'

'Oh, lots of things. Lots of things. A device for keeping bathwater hot for a start. He does most of his inventing in the bath. And lots more. His latest invention is a digital sundial. It's sure to make him another zillion denarii. And that gives him big tax problems.'

'And Messrs Cursus & Minimis are busy solving those problems right now?'

'Yes. They are probably advising him to invest in the Egyptian Pyramid Company.'

'And what do they do?'

'Sell pyramids to the Egyptians.'

'But the Egyptians have already got lots of pyramids!'

'Precisely, sir.'

'But a company like that must lose a lot of money!'

'Oh camel-loads of money, sir. The company is a long way in the red. Thus it is a very useful tax write-off. To balance against the profitable investments, you see, and reduce the taxable income.'

'In other words, a tax scam. And that's what's keeping Cursus & Minimis so busy just at the moment?'

'That's right, sir. And so we couldn't possibly disturb them.'

'Perhaps you can answer some questions for us then,' suggested Rachel.

'I'll try, if you like,' said Subservius, hesitantly.

'Do you remember a young woman named Abigail Jacobson?'

'Oh yes, of course I do. She used to work here before Julia.'

'Who is Julia?'

'Julia the Junior. You met her in the outer office. What's happened to Abigail?'

'She's been murdered.'

'Murdered? But that's terrible.'

'Yes, it's very sad.'

'Sad? It's more than sad! It's terrible! It probably means bad luck for everyone who knew her!' (I had forgotten just how superstitious these Romans were.)

'Mind you, it's a long time since I've known her,' continued Subservius, talking more to himself than to us. 'Perhaps only a little of the bad luck will rub off on me.'

'Just how long is it?' I asked.

'Eh?'

'Just how long since Abigail worked here?'

'About a year, I guess.'

'How well did you know her?'

'She was hard to get to know. Very quiet. Very reserved. Didn't talk much.'

'Did she ever talk about her interests outside the office?'

'She didn't talk much at all.'

'Did she mention boyfriends, hobbies, interests? Think about it carefully: any hint we get might help us track down a murderer.'

'You don't think her murder has anything to do with this office, do you?' asked Subservius nervously. 'It can't have! No. It can't have. I mean, it's a year since she worked here.'

'We know it's unlikely,' I explained patiently, 'but we have to check out all the angles.'

'So,' said Rachel, taking up the questioning, 'did she have any boyfriends, any hobbies, any outside interests when you knew her?'

Subservius seemed to think about this carefully before answering. 'I can't think of anything. Honestly I can't. Really, when I think back, I think she was very young for her age.'

'Meaning what, exactly?'

'Just that she wasn't very interested in the things that most young women of her age are interested in.'

'Such as?'

'Well...she didn't seem very interested in young men, for a start. Now, as an accountant I can tell you that the one thing a young woman of Abigail's age should be thinking about is marriage. That's where financial security can be found. Especially if you have a tight pre-nuptial agreement.'

'And Abigail wasn't interested?'

'Not a bit! I gave her some fatherly advice along those lines, but she didn't pay attention. I mean to say, we have some pretty rich clients coming in here from time to time, and some of them have moderately agreeable sons. And I used to say to Abigail, "Speak to these young men. Take this opportunity to get to know people with money. Be nice to them." But she wasn't interested.'

'Perhaps because she was Jewish?'

'Maybe. I don't know anything about the Jewish religion. All I know is that young Abigail should have been interested in marrying money, and wasn't. She was immature.'

'Are you saying that she wasn't intelligent?'

'Oh no. She was bright enough. And very curious with it. There was nothing wrong with her brains.'

'But there were no boyfriends, no hobbies, no outside interests?'

'That's what I'm telling you. She was a quiet kid who kept her head down and got on with the job.'

'Why did she leave?'

'She got a better job, that's all — up at the palace.'

'Could either Mr Cursus or Mr Minimis tell us anything about Abigail that you might have missed?'

'I can answer that in two words: im-possible. She reported directly to me. I knew her much better than them.'

'In that case,' I said, 'our business here is complete. Thank you for your time, Mr Subservius.'

The senior clerk started leading us to the door, a matter of only three steps in that tiny office, then stopped and said thoughtfully: 'I've just remembered.'

'Remembered what?' asked Rachel.

'There was one outside interest she had. There was one thing she used to ask me about.'

'And what was that?'

'Religion. She used to ask me about Roman religion. For a Jew she was strangely interested in what we Romans do for religion.'

'What did you tell her?'

'I explained that I made a point of popping into all the important temples from time to time. Jupiter, Mars, Venus, Minerva, Mercury, Diana, Vulcan — I'd call into all of them from time to time. You've got to keep the gods on-side if you want good luck. So I'd get around to all of them, a little offering here, a little offering there. That sort of thing. And I'd consult the staff fortune teller at each of the temples. Believe what you wish, keep your head down, don't get into trouble, and have good luck — that's what life's all about. And that's what I used to tell Abigail.'

Rachel and I exchanged a glance. Clearly Abigail's search for meaning, for truth, went back a long way.

'Well, thanks for all your help, Mr Subservius,' said Rachel, and we both shook his hand.

Chapter 24

'So much for Cursus & Minimis,' said Rachel, as we clambered down the rickety wooden stairs and back out into the street. 'I suppose it's time to visit the funeral directors?'

We found the premises of 'De Mortuis' on the opposite side of the Forum: an impressive-looking shop front, all fake marble pillars and heavy, black drapes.

Stepping inside, we found ourselves in a large, dimly lit, echoing chamber. Around us were open caskets and coffins on display, illuminated by the flickering light from numerous funeral lamps.

Out of the gloom two shapes loomed up towards us.

'May we be of service to you?' said the first, in a lachrymose voice. 'I'm Mr Smith, and this is Mr Jones.'

With my eyes rapidly adjusting to the dim light I could see that these two morticians looked remarkably like each other. Both were middle-aged, overweight, and balding. Both had fat, greedy hands, greasy smiles, and oily voices — the verbal equivalent of dripping slime.

'We can offer any kind of funeral service,' continued Mr Smith (or was it Mr Jones?).

'Any religion, any nationality,' added Mr Jones (or possibly Mr Smith).

'We offer burial in catacombs, crypts…'

'…tombs and pyramids. We can offer for the Loved One a coffin, or casket…'

'…or our Super Sarcophagus, handpainted with all modern conveniences.'

I glanced at Rachel. She was shivering and looking decidedly uncomfortable. I didn't blame her.

'I'm Ben Bartholomew. This is my wife Rachel. We're private detectives, and we're here to ask some questions.'

'Oh, I'm not so sure about that. Are you, Mr Jones?'

'Certainly not, Mr Smith! It's an investigation, isn't it? Do we want to be involved in an investigation?'

'I should say not! So, there is your answer, and we suggest you leave our premises immediately!'

'This is a murder investigation,' I said firmly. 'We've been retained by the victim's family, and we're not leaving here until we've got a few answers.'

'Murder, did they say, Mr Jones?'

'…yes, Mr Smith, murder. And who is the poor unfortunate victim, if we may ask?'

'Her name is Abigail Jacobson,' said Rachel.

'Abigail Jacobson? I seem to know that name, Mr Jones. Didn't we once employ…'

'…someone by that name? Yes, Mr Smith, I rather think we did. She was a junior clerk, out the back, in the office.'

'That's why we're here,' I explained. 'We want to ask you about Abigail. If we can find out more about her, perhaps that will give us a lead on her killer.'

'Ah, we understand now, don't we, Mr Jones?'

'We certainly do, Mr Smith. And if we may ask a question…?'

'Certainly,' I replied.

'Have Miss Abigail's funeral requirements been met? I mean to say, have the *arrangements* been made?'

'Not yet. The coroner has not yet released the body.'

'Ah, well, in that case…would you be kind enough to inform the next of kin that the firm of De Mortuis would be honoured to take care of the necessary arrangements for the Loved One…'

'…at a special price, of course, Mr Smith.'

'Oh, yes, of course, Mr Jones! Seeing as how the Loved One once worked here.'

'We'll pass on the message to her family,' I said. 'Now — a few questions.'

'Go right ahead…'

'…yes, right ahead. Ask whatever you wish.'

'What was Abigail like when she worked here?'

'What was she like? How would you describe her, Mr Jones?'

'Oh, quiet, Mr Smith. That's the word I would use — quiet.'

'The very word! Yes, that's the word I would use too — she was very quiet. Reserved. Even *shy* when she worked for us.'

'She didn't talk about her private life at all? Did any friends ever come to meet her after work?' asked Rachel.

'I certainly never saw any. I think she was a rather solitary child, with very few friends to speak of. Would you agree, Mr Jones?'

'Totally, Mr Smith. I can recall no instance of any person calling here for Abigail.'

'Did she have any interests? Or hobbies?'

'It's so hard to say. She was so quiet, you see. I can't recall her conversations very well at all. There were so few of them, weren't there, Mr Smith?'

'Very few indeed, Mr Jones. Although I do recall one occasion…now let me see. Ah, yes. It was in our embalming room one afternoon. I was working on a Loved One there…'

'….he's very good at embalming is Mr Smith. Very artistic, in fact.'

'It's very kind of you to say so, Mr Jones, very kind indeed. Now, where was I? Ah, yes. I was working in the embalming room and Abigail came in with a message. She stayed to watch me work for a few minutes, and then she began to ask me questions.'

'What sort of questions?' I asked.

'About the point of death. And what different religions had to say about death. She wanted to know why the Greeks placed a coin under the tongue of the Loved One to pay the ferryman. And why some prefer pyramids and others funeral pyres.'

'And what did you tell her?'

'I told her that the point of death was to keep us in business. That's right, isn't it, Mr Jones?'

'It certainly is, Mr Smith. But you musn't mind us, Mr and Mrs Bartholomew — that's just our little joke. We really do have the greatest sympathy with the next of kin of the Loved One.'

'After your little joke — what else did you tell Abigail?'

'I told her that my own personal view is…well, a view that I share with Mr Jones, actually…is that death is the end of it all. So the important thing, I explained, is to go out with a bang. A really big funeral show to wrap it all up — that's how every life should end.'

'Did Rachel respond to that at all?'

'Only to ask more questions. If death is the end, what's the purpose of it all? Where is meaning to be found? Where is truth to be found? I told her she was straining her brain, and I chased her back to the office.'

'Much the best thing to do in the circumstances, Mr Smith,' said Mr Jones (I was starting to sort them out by now), 'much the best. No point in asking too many questions, no point at all.'

I glanced at Rachel and she glanced at me. She raised an eyebrow, and I nodded in response — just the slightest of nods.

'Well, I think that's all, gentlemen,' I said. 'Thank you for your co-operation.'

'Anything we can do to help...'

'....at any time. Don't hesitate to call on us. And don't forget to mention us to the next of kin...'

'....give them our sympathy, and offer them a special price, in light of our...our...'

'...our previous connection with the Loved One.'

Back outside the funeral parlour, as we made our way through the dust and crowds of the Forum, Rachel remarked, 'It's odd, really.'

'What's odd?' I asked.

'That a Jewish girl would work in a funeral parlour like that. Touching a dead body would have made her ritually unclean, and she couldn't have gone to synagogue.'

'True. But she worked in the office, remember. I doubt that she ever touched a dead body in the whole time she worked there. Smith and Jones seem to do that side of the work personally.'

'And *enjoy* doing it!' said Rachel with a shiver.

'But there is one thing I wonder about.'

'And what's that?'

'I am wondering if that is where it all started.'

'Where what all started?'

'Abigail's search. I wonder whether being made daily aware of the reality of death started her on her quest.'

Rachel agreed that it may have been the start of the whole thing, and we made our way slowly and thoughtfully back to our apartment.

The big disappointment when we got back home was the mail. The response to my newspaper advertisement about The Haunted Temple was — zilch, zero, nought, nil, nothing.

'Perhaps it is such a secretive temple that very few people know about it,' suggested Rachel.

'Or perhaps it is so secretive that the people who do know are too terrified to say anything,' I responded.

Then I dialled the number of my old newspaper friend, Petronius Laconicus. But he also had no news.

'Sorry, Ben old chum,' he said, 'I've made enquiries in so many bars that you probably owe me a liver transplant, but the answer is always the same: no one has ever heard of The Haunted Temple.'

All of which was no help at all.

'What if,' said Rachel thoughtfully, when I told her Laconicus' news — or lack of news, 'what if The Haunted Temple is not the true name of the place?'

'I don't follow?'

'What if The Haunted Temple is just Abigail's own name for the place — a kind of nickname — and the real name of the last temple on her list is something else entirely.'

'Great! Now instead of looking for a missing temple, we have to look for an *unnamed* missing temple! I don't know how that helps at all.'

'Sorry. I was only trying to help.'

'Look, you may be right, sweetheart, but what I need now is a clue that really helps. I think I'll go back to that bar, the Ipso Vino, and have another word with that dumb ox of a man who hangs around all the temples.'

'Vacuus?'

'Yes. He may have heard something about The Haunted Temple since the last time I spoke to him.'

But if he had found out something, I never learned what it was.

Vacuus had disappeared.

At least, that's what his friend Maximus, the bartender, told me.

The Ipso Vino bar and grill looked exactly as it had the first time I called in there: the same card-players, the same dim, smoky atmosphere. The only difference was that Vacuus was missing from his usual corner table.

'I haven't seen him for two days,' said Maximus.

'Did he say he might be going away somewhere?' I asked.

'Not to me, he didn't.'

'Has he ever disappeared like this before?'

'Never. He practically lives in this place. Has done for years.'

'Any idea what might have happened to him?'

'None. But I'll tell you this free, gratis and for nothing,' said Maximus as he leaned across the bar and dropped his voice to a low whisper. 'That dumb ox is a friend of mine, and I'm worried — very worried!'

CHAPTER 25

The next morning I decided to do what I used to do in the old days, when I was a full-time private investigator — write up my case notes. The task was a long one, and took me until after lunch.

Sometimes putting all the information down on paper sorts out my thinking, and helps me to locate those small clues I might otherwise overlook. But on this occasion I found the more I wrote, the foggier my thinking became. And if there were any hidden clues, instead of leaping out at me they hid themselves even more deeply in the morass of detail.

While I was sitting at the dining-room table writing, there was a loud knock at the front door.

'I'll get it,' said Rachel, and hurried downstairs.

A few moments later I heard Rachel's delighted squeal of 'Peter! What are you doing here? It's wonderful to see you! Come in! Come in!'

Then there was a loud clatter of feet on the stairs, and suddenly our tiny lounge-cum-dining room seemed to be full of people.

In the middle of the group, and towering over them — on account of his height, his flaming red hair and beard, and booming voice — was Peter, who was now leader of the followers of Jesus.

Amidst the babble of voices and introductions I learned that the men travelling with Peter were named Timon, Justus and Aeneas and that Peter was on his way to the house of Captain Cornelius!

So, the message from Cornelius to Peter had worked! You could have knocked me over with a feather!

Momma bustled around serving everyone drinks, and Peter told us to sit down, while he explained the remarkable things that had happened in the last forty-eight hours.

Peter explained that, the day before yesterday, he had had a vision in which God had assured him that the message of hope, and a fresh start, in Jesus Christ was a message for all the nations — not just the Jewish people. Immediately after this vision, Cornelius' messengers had arrived. Peter had given them food and accommodation overnight, and then set out with them for Caesarea.

The big ex-fisherman went on to explain that he was on his way to Cornelius' house now, stopping on the way to collect us and Philip, the only Christians he knew living in Caesarea.

Peter was clearly in a hurry, so we finished our drinks and set out as a group, picking up Philip on the way.

Captain Cornelius lived in a typical Roman villa in one of the northern beach suburbs of Caesarea. Our friend had just enough rank to have done reasonably well out of the Roman army staff housing department. It was a large, white stucco villa, dripping with terracotta — roof tiles, downpipes, waterspouts, all were decorated terracotta.

When we were admitted I was surprised to find the atrium of the villa already filled with people. These, it turned out, were family and friends of

Cornelius, invited by him to hear what Peter had to say.

The behaviour of Captain Cornelius himself was, I am bound to say, fairly embarrassing. As Peter entered the porch, Cornelius fell on his knees in an attitude of worship!

But Peter was having none of this.

'Stand up!' said Peter, 'I'm a man, and only a man, no different from you!'

So Cornelius got up and he and Peter talked quietly together as they made their way into the courtyard where the rest of us were assembled.

Peter stood beside a table at one end of the courtyard, cleared his throat, and began to speak.

'You know it is against the Jewish laws for me to come into a non-Jewish home like this,' he said, 'but God has shown me in a vision that I should never think of anyone as inferior. So I came as soon as I was sent for. Now tell me what you want.'

Cornelius explained about the vision he had experienced, and how, and why he had sent for Peter.

Peter rubbed his beard thoughtfully, and then said: 'I see very clearly now that God doesn't play favourites! In every nation God has his hand on those people who fear him and do what is right. It makes no difference who you are or where you're from: if you want God and are ready to do as he says, the door is open. The message that he sent first to the Jews (that through Jesus Christ everything is being put together again), well, now he's sending that message everywhere among everyone.'

Peter went on to tell the people the story of Jesus, of the life he lived, the things he taught, and the death he died at the hands of the authorities. But that was not the end of it, Peter said. The God who made the universe brought Jesus back to life again, as proof that this Jesus is God's appointed ruler of the world and judge of all people.

Through Jesus, Peter explained, God offers forgiveness, and friendship, and a place in his family. Cornelius and the members of his household welcomed this news gladly. And when it was obvious that God had accepted these people, Peter insisted that we must accept them too, and baptised them.

Afterwards Cornelius begged Peter and his group to stay with him at his house for a few days; Peter agreed.

As we walked back home Rachel and I could not stop talking about what we had seen and heard.

'What strikes me,' I said, 'is that they are two such different people.'

'Who are?' asked Rachel.

'Peter and Cornelius.'

'Yes...I suppose they are, really.'

'Cornelius is wealthy, a non-Jew, and a military man, while Peter is a Jewish fisherman-turned-preacher.'

'True. And God's plan includes both of them.'

'Not only includes them, but includes them *together*. Today a Jewish Christian leader and a brand new non-Jewish Christian have discovered something significant about God at work in the other person.'

'You're saying that Peter and Cornelius, in a sense, needed each other?'

'Yes. In God's plan each learned something from the other.'

'Specifically?'

'Specifically, Cornelius needed Peter and his message to know he could be rescued from the mess this world is in — that the gap between him and God is bridged by Jesus. While Peter needed Cornelius and his dramatic experience to know that non-Jews are included in God's plan.'

'And it all is God's plan, isn't it?'

'Indeed it is. It is God who has given Cornelius and his family a hunger for Himself, and it is God who then satisfied that hunger by giving them the ability to turn to Him.'

CHAPTER 26

Rachel and I sat up late that night, talking and drinking coffee. It was well after midnight before we finally fell asleep.

I was deeply asleep and dreaming. It was a strange dream in which I was surrounded by haunted temples, when suddenly all of the bells in all of the temples started to ring simultaneously. It was a hideous, frightful din!

Slowly I struggled into consciousness: the ringing sound I could hear was the telephone.

I willed my feet to swing out of the sheets and onto the floor. I was astonished when they obeyed me. I tried it again: upright! I told myself. And a moment later I was swaying a little unsteadily, but standing upright beside the bed, nevertheless.

I glanced at Rachel: she had not stirred.

In an attempt to stop the telephone from waking her I hurried my uncoordinated limbs downstairs, arriving with a slightly surprised thump at the bottom. I stumbled towards the phone without turning on the light (I didn't want to add being dazzled to being uncoordinated and confused), and silently cursing Alexander Graham Bell and his odious invention, I grabbed the handset.

'Hello, who's calling?' I said.

No, I tell a lie. That's what I *tried* to say. What actually came out was something more like: 'Lo?

oooh aaah…?' Apparently my mouth was not yet coordinated with my brain.

'Is that you, Ben?' asked the telephone.

Who else could it be? Had I been woken up at this hour to ask if I was me?

'Uh huh,' I replied wittily, making it clear that I was ready for a heavy intellectual exchange.

'It's Laconicus here.'

Silence at my end while I tried to register this.

'Petronius Laconicus,' explained the telephone, 'I'm working the overnight shift on the sub's desk at the newspaper. A report's just come in that I thought you ought to know about.'

I shook my head. A few cobwebs blew away and a little dust settled.

'Tell me about it,' I slurred.

'You sound half-asleep,' said Laconicus.

'Make that three-quarters. No, nine-tenths. On second thoughts, forget the fraction — what's the news?'

'A dead body has just been found. And when I read the report I thought of you.'

'Who's dead?'

'That guy I put you on to, the odd-job man around all the temples — Vacuus. He's been murdered.'

'Vacuus? Oh, yeah, sure, him. Murdered?'

'That's right. His body was discovered about an hour ago by the city watch. I thought it might have something to do with your case. And if so, I thought you might like to get down to the scene of the crime before everything's shifted.'

'Well, you could be right at that. What time is it?'

'Two o'clock.'

'Two o'clock *in the morning*?'

'Take a look outside, Ben — it's pitch dark.'

I did, he was right.

'I've had less than two hours' sleep!' I complained.

'I'm sorry for waking you, old chum,' said Laconicus, 'I just thought it might be useful, that's all.'

'No...no...you're right. I'd better go and check it out. Where was the body found?'

'Down on the docks. Near pier 17. Our crime reporter is down there already. His name is Crispus. He can fill you in on the details.'

'Thanks. Thanks for calling,' I muttered as I scribbled down the address.

I called the all-night cab company and ordered a cab. Five minutes, I was told. Then I pulled on a fresh tunic and sandals, splashed water over my face to wake me up, and pulled a cloak around my shoulders.

I crept upstairs to sneak a look at Rachel. She was still sleeping like a baby, and I decided not to disturb her.

I hurried as quietly as I could down the stairs and out into the street, and found the cab waiting.

'I didn't hear you arrive,' I said, as I climbed up beside the driver.

'This hour of the night we have the horses' hooves muffled,' he explained, 'so as not to disturb the sleeping citizenry.'

'Very considerate.'

'Not our idea. It's a new city regulation. That's all these Roman governors are good for — inventing new regulations. I can remember what it was like when I was a kid...'

That's all I needed: a gabby cabby!

I ignored the flow of words, and inhaled the cool salty night air. Within a few minutes I was fully awake and fully alert.

As we approached pier 17 there could be no mistaking my destination. The floodlights were set up, and a crowd of officers were moving around in the pool of light like moths restlessly fluttering around a candle.

I paid off the cab and walked over to the group.

They were mainly young city watch officers, although I also recognised the driver of the mortuary wagon and his offsider. And crouched over the body in the centre of the group was the forensic pathologist, Dr Nostrum.

Standing back a little way, where he could get the full light of a flood lamp on his notebook, and scribbling away furiously in that notebook, was a young man. I approached him.

'You Crispus?' I asked.

'That's me.'

'I'm Bartholomew — Ben Bartholomew. A friend of Petronius Laconicus.'

'Yes, he told me you might turn up.'

'Can you tell me what's happened here?'

'There's not much to tell. Around midnight a watchman who works at that warehouse over there was on his way to work. He saw some sort of movement down here by the wharf. When he came over to investigate, someone dropped a heavy load and ran off. The heavy load turned out to be the body.'

'I see. I suppose he didn't get a good look at the guy who ran off?'

'You suppose right. A dark figure, that's all he told us.'

'Nothing else?'

'Average height, average build. It's pretty dark

around here, you can hardly blame the watchman. Oh, there was one thing, though...'

'Yes?'

'He reckoned that whoever it was, wasn't very fit. He was grunting and puffing when he was trying to move the body, and when he ran off it was a limping, exhausted run.'

'So, an unfit murderer dumps a dead body here at midnight. And that's all we know?'

'Just about.'

Crispus went back to scribbling in his notebook. I shouldered my way through the group and took a look at the corpse.

Vacuus looked quite peaceful in death.

Until, that is, Dr Nostrum rolled the body over. The back of his head did not look peaceful at all. It was a pulverised mess of dried blood.

'That what killed him?' I asked.

'Looks like it,' replied Dr Nostrum over his shoulder, without turning around to see who was asking the questions. 'I'll know more after the autopsy.'

'How long has he been dead?'

'First guess: around twenty-four hours.'

'What sort of weapon did that damage?'

'Your classic blunt instrument, I would say. An iron bar, the handle of spear — something of that sort. He was struck three times. The first blow killed him, the other two were just to make sure.'

'How was he struck?'

'From below. That is to say, by someone shorter than the victim.'

'That doesn't tell us much,' I muttered, 'since everyone is shorter than that big ox of a man.'

'Oh, yes,' added the doctor, showing off I suspect.

'And the murderer was almost certainly right-handed.'

'A right-handed person of average height. Thanks doc, that helps a lot!'

I took one last look at Vacuus, lying there like a bull in a slaughterhouse, and pushed my way out of the circle of peering faces.

At the edge of the group I came face to face with the young city watch officer we had met when Abigail's body had been found.

'Hi,' he said, recognising me.

'Hi,' I responded, and then, needing something obvious and fatuous to say, added, 'another grisly one.'

'Certainly is.'

'What do you think happened?' I asked, not because I particularly wanted his opinion, but because I was making conversation.

'Well, the doc says he wasn't murdered here, and he's been dead for a day. And when you add that to the evidence of the nightwatchman, I'd say his body was being disposed of by the murderer.'

Well, ask an obvious question, get an obvious answer.

'I would guess,' he continued, 'that the nightwatchman disturbed him before he finished what he came down here to the docks to do.'

'And what was that?' I asked, feeding him his straight line (always encourage these youngsters to think, that's my policy).

'Drop the body off the end of the pier. But it's a big, heavy body, and was slow to move, and he panicked and ran away when the nightwatchman disturbed him.'

Which is exactly what I had concluded after my talk with Crispus.

I hung around the docks until they removed the body, but I didn't discover any further information.

By the time I decided to head back to my nice warm bed, the first dull, grey light of dawn was pushing though the clouds in the eastern sky. I decided to walk rather than try to find a cab at this hour.

I walked slowly, pulling the cloak around my shoulders to keep out the morning cold and damp. And as I walked, I thought.

Did this death have anything to do with the Abigail Jacobson murder case? Possibly not, of course. But more likely it did.

Had my inquiries stirred up some dust, put the cat among the pigeons, and assorted other clichés? Was Vacuus in some way involved in the Abigail Jacobson case? Had that led to his death? And what did the mysterious Haunted Temple have to do with it all?

Chapter 27

Our house was still locked up and in darkness when I arrived home. Standing on the front doorstep, digging through my pockets, I discovered that I did not have the house keys with me.

I stood back and stared at the locked door, and at the closed and silent windows. Somewhere inside there, I thought, are my house keys — probably lying on the table beside my bed. Only a few metres away. But there was no way I could get them without waking up Rachel and Momma.

A cold, gusty wind whistled around the corner and rattled the leaves on the cobblestones.

I pulled my cloak tighter. They need their sleep, I decided. I would find an early-opening coffee house and have some hot coffee and hot rolls, and then return when they had woken up. That's what I decided.

Some decisions can be awfully dumb!

You see, it was only after I had consumed several hot rolls and two cups of hot coffee that I realised that my wallet was also missing from my pocket. Probably lying beside my keys on the same bedside table.

The waiter who had served me was one of the those large, dark Italians whose five o'clock shadow starts at five o'clock in the morning.

'Excuse me,' I said, rather nervously, 'I know this

is going to sound very silly, and I certainly feel very foolish, but you see — I've left my wallet at home.'

'Huh?' he growled. (He knew perfectly well what I had said, but he was making me spell it out.)

'I have no money to pay for the coffee and rolls,' I said bluntly.

'So, you're one of those, are you?'

'One of what?'

'A sponger! A grafter! I've come across your kind before. And I know how to deal with you!' As he spoke he was rolling up the sleeves of his shirt.

'You're not threatening me with physical violence are you?' I spluttered. 'I thought the Italians were civilised.'

'That's the Greeks. You're confusing us with the Greeks!'

'Sorry...don't take offence.'

He said nothing, but grabbed my arm and pulled me to my feet. 'Gino — give me a hand,' he growled.

Gino gave him a hand by grabbing my other arm.

With a big, solidly built Italian waiter on either side of me I was marched towards the back of the café. Oh, great! I thought, they're going beat me up in a back alley.

But they didn't.

When we got to the kitchen they released my arms, flung a tea-towel into my hands, and said: 'Get to work. About an hour's washing and wiping up should pay for your breakfast.'

For a moment I stood there like an idiot staring at the tea-towel and considering my options. I suppose I could have telephoned home, woken up Rachel, and told her to come straight down to the café with my wallet. But I had gone to such lengths to let her sleep, why spoil it now? I looked at the pile of dirty dishes, and started work.

An hour later all I wanted to do was go back to sleep. As I trudged wearily back towards our little home I did the sums in my head: I had woken up at 2 a.m., after just two hours' sleep; I had spent several hours on my feet at the scene of the murder; I had walked back home, walked down to the café, and then done an hour's work in the kitchen. And what did all that add up to? Back to bed. That's what.

I knocked on my own front door, and, as I stood there waiting for it to open, it started to rain. Early in the morning, I found, that light, misty Mediterranean rain was freezing cold — as cold as a cave in the Arctic ice! I pulled my cloak up to shelter my head and waited.

At last the lock clicked and the door swung open, and there stood Rachel in her dressing gown.

'Ben! Where have you been? I didn't hear you get up and leave. Come in quickly, you look half-frozen, you poor thing.'

The only nice thing, I discovered, about arriving home disguised as a frozen waif is the sympathy and cuddles you get from your wife.

As I scrubbed myself clean over a hot tub of water I told Rachel about my adventures of the night. My adventures in the Italian café, I'm afraid to say, reduced her to a helpless fit of the giggles. Some women have a strange way of displaying sympathy.

On the matter of the murder of Vacuus, however, she was much more serious. 'Why would anyone want a harmless oaf of a man like that dead?' she asked.

'Not harmless,' I gurgled as I splashed hot water

over my head. 'Not harmless to someone — that's why he's dead.'

'I suppose so. But why was he killed?'

'My guess is that he knew too much. In his slow-thinking way, he may finally have put the pieces together and decided that he knew something worth suppressing.'

'Yes! Of course! And he may then have decided to go into business on his own account: the business of blackmail.'

'Two minds with but a single thought. That's the conclusion I had come to. Pass me that towel, will you please, sweetheart?'

'So what are we going to do next?'

'I don't know about you, but I am going back to bed. I am just about ready to drop, and I would like a few hours' sleep at least before I make any plans.'

Five minutes later I was in bed, and ten minutes later I was sound asleep.

My sleep was very restless, punctuated by a recurring dream.

In my dream I was surrounded not by one haunted temple, but many. And among the temples were the ghostly figures of Lamas and Clockmakers and other assorted gurus. And they were all beckoning me into what they called 'the most haunted temple of all' — a dark, ominous temple, as black as coal and gleaming like polished ebony. I didn't want to go in, but they propelled me towards the doors that swung open to greet me — like the jaws of a shark. And inside I found that the temple was indeed haunted — by the ghost of Abigail Jacobson. I turned and tried to run away, but my feet wouldn't move. I looked down and discovered that I was being gripped tightly around the ankles by the gigantic ghost of Vacuus. I struggled against his grip, and struggled some more.

And then I woke up, in a lather of sweat, with the sheets twisted around my feet.

Dressed in fresh clothes I came downstairs from the bedroom to find Rachel and Momma seated around our tiny kitchen table doing the beans together. Rachel was stringing the beans, and Momma was slicing them.

'Ah, you're up at last, sleepy-head,' said Rachel. 'You realise you've missed the best part of the day?'

'Coffee. Please,' was all I could manage, 'I need to clear my head.'

'That's what your sleep was supposed to do for you, Benjamin my boy,' said Momma. 'I could have told you it wouldn't work. I've always said that sleeping late is unhealthy. A mother knows these things.'

'Yes, Momma,' I murmured. 'Any phone calls? Has the mail come?'

'Yes,' said Rachel as she put the coffee pot on the stove, 'the mail has come. And before you ask your next question, no — there was no reply to our Haunted Temple advertisement.'

I must have pulled a sour face at that news because Momma remarked, 'Don't make faces like that, my boy. It might get stuck, and you'd have to live with that face for the rest of your life! How would you like them apples, eh?'

'Have you heard from Poppa in Jerusalem lately?' I asked between clenched teeth.

'I spoke to your dear Poppa on the telephone this morning,' gushed Momma. 'He is such a worrier, that man; such an awful worrier. He wants that I should come home at once, what with all these killings and stabbings and bashings going on all the time.'

Momma managed to make it sound as if there were a fresh corpse on the door-step every morning.

'So you told him you'd go straight back home to Jerusalem, did you?' I asked hopefully.

'Of course not!' Momma was outraged. 'I told him that I would stay with my Benjamin and my Rachel until I was sure they were out of danger.'

'Really, Momma, there's no need,' I protested. 'It's not as if there's anything you could actually do.'

'Do, shmoo. Don't argue! I'm staying until the danger is past. I'm your mother: what else can I do? Besides which, while you two are out being attacked, and assaulted and threatened and I don't know what else, someone has to sit here and worry about you. That's what I do. Nobody does it better.'

'And what about calls?' I said, turning to Rachel as she handed me a cup of coffee. 'You said there had been phone calls.'

'Two. One from Philip reminding us of the meeting at his place tomorrow morning...'

'Right. And the other one?'

'From Lord Weekly's secretary at The Inner Temple, repeating the invitation for us to attend the seminar being given tonight by Hortensia Ignorantias.'

'Seminar?' said Momma. 'You two wouldn't go to a seminar at that place, would you? It has a bad odour about it. A mother can tell these things.'

'Momma...'

'You have to be sensible, that's what you have to do!'

'Momma, Rachel and I don't disagree with what you say. In fact, we agree absolutely. But we have to go as part of our investigation.'

CHAPTER 28

When we arrived at The Inner Temple that night we discovered that we were not to be part of a small select group. Select perhaps, but certainly not small.

The parking lot was full of expensive imported foreign chariots, and the double doors leading to the entrance lobby were bulging as a well-dressed crowd shuffled forward in an orderly queue some ten people wide.

'Ben! I didn't realise people were coming dressed like this!'

'Dressed like what?' I asked.

'Men! You're so unobservant. Look at this crowd. They're all in formal wear. They look like they're going to the opera!'

'Yes, yes, so they do. I guess you're right.'

'And look how I'm dressed — how *we're* dressed.'

'Well, what about it? Our clothes are clean and well pressed. What's wrong?'

'We are not in formal tunics — that's what's wrong,' insisted Rachel. 'I feel like the tramp who wandered into the ballroom. I don't think I can go in. I'd rather go home than go inside dressed like this.'

'Look. This is a murder investigation, not a fashion show. Okay, so we've neglected to wear our best togas and our dark cloaks. And some of this well-heeled mob may look down their noses at us. But so what? If we pick up some clues to Abigail's murder, what other people think is irrelevant.'

'I suppose you're right,' said Rachel, but she didn't sound convinced.

The lobby did indeed look like opera night at the Colosseum, with the reception desk transformed into a box office. I elbowed my way through the crowd.

When we eventually got to the counter I said: 'Ben and Rachel Bartholomew. There should be some tickets here for us. We are guests of Lord Weekly.'

'Just a moment, sir,' said the fluttery young woman behind the desk.

She sorted through a small pile of envelopes, and then found one bearing our names. 'Here you are, sir,' she said. 'Enjoy the evening.'

As I backed away from the crowded counter I noticed the large piles of denarii and shekels being paid by others, and I was glad that our tickets were complimentaries — this was clearly a very expensive affair.

As we shuffled into the auditorium, shoulder to shoulder with the other members of the audience, I became aware of their satin robes and our cotton ones, their brushed velvet cloaks and our woollen ones, and the men's silk cravats and the women's fur stoles, and I could understand Rachel's point.

As a uniformed usherette led us to our numbered seats I whispered to Rachel, 'All we need now is a bag of popcorn and a glossy program.'

'It is rather more like theatre than religion, isn't it?' giggled Rachel.

The evening performance (well, what else can I call it?) began with some soft and lyrical 'ambient' music played by a small jazz combo. As they played, the lights dimmed and slides of God's creation at its most beautiful were projected onto a giant screen: golden sunrises, glowing sunsets, flowers, forests, beaches and oceans.

This part of the performance came to end, and was rewarded with polite applause.

Then a deep voice boomed at us over the loudspeakers: 'Ladies and gentlemen, would you please welcome the world's leading Enlightened Soul, bestselling author and lecturer...Hortensia Ignorantias!'

The applause that followed was rapturous. It thundered on for several minutes while deep-red velvet curtains parted and Hortensia made her way, in a slow and stately fashion, to the front of the stage.

There was, as I had noticed before, something larger than life about Hortensia: the bold slash of scarlet lipstick, the massive froth of red curly hair that surrounded her face. She was dressed in many layers of brightly coloured swirling silk, and a necklace of extraordinarily large pearls encircled her white throat.

She looked almost exactly the same as when we'd met her. Almost, but not quite. Although Rachel and I had an excellent view from our seats near the front, I could not work out just what was different about Hortensia's appearance.

I put the problem to one side as she started to speak: 'Dear, dear friends. I am here tonight to tell you that every human being is a god. The human self and the divine self, they are one. I am a god: you are a god. Turn to the god within for the highest ethic, the highest morality of all: self-fulfilment.'

'How convenient,' whispered Rachel.

'Yes — if you are a god you can make your own rules and nobody can argue with you,' I replied.

'Sssshh!' hissed someone in the row behind us, so we stopped our whispered conversation.

'Your mind is getting in the way,' Hortensia was saying. 'Don't evaluate. Don't judge. Don't think. Just experience. Just let it happen. Your experiences are divine.' She paused for effect. 'Dear friends, someone said to me the other day, "With all due respect, Hortensia, I don't think you are a god." And I immediately replied, "If you don't see me as God, it's because you don't see yourself as God." '

I looked around me at all these well-dressed, well-off, but otherwise quite ordinary people. I wanted to say to each one of them: what privileges does being a god confer? Does it make you immune from unemployment, from suffering or pain? From death? What hope does it give you, in the face of the present reality of suffering and the future event of death?

While I was thinking these things, Hortensia had gone on to talk about 'near-death' experiences. She talked about people she had met who, under the surgeon's knife or during a serious illness, had come within a whisker of death. They all, apparently, reported seeing things like bright lights, and experiencing a feeling of warmth. But none of the reports concerned experiences of death, or of what exists after death. They were simply perceptions of what seemed to happen close to death.

But what if someone were to die, really die, I thought, and return from the dead to tell us about the experience of death, and what lies beyond? Would not this witness be of first-rate importance? Would it not possess an authority far and above Hortensia's tales of 'near-death' experiences? Would we not pay attention to such a person? I had investigated the resurrection of Jesus in detail.* I knew he was that person.

Hortensia was building up to a big finish. 'The realm of transcendent knowing,' she thundered, 'is that of which I speak. Beyond reason. Beyond words. You must be willing to have experiences and not have words for them.'

I was somewhat surprised that while Hortensia was speaking, the lights in the auditorium had been left turned fully on. I would have thought that the rules of good showmanship required the lights to be dimmed and Hortensia to stand in a spotlight. Instead of which, we were listening to her under a blaze of white light.

Then I discovered the reason why.

'Now, dear friends,' she announced, 'I am going to attempt to summon up my guiding spirit: Tantalus. I would ask for your complete silence, please. No noise, and no movement, please; nothing that will break my concentration.'

So saying, she closed her eyes, threw her head back and her arms out, and began to moan — softly at first, but gradually louder. Slowly her whole body began to tremble and shake.

Suddenly the lights went out.

From blazing white light we were plunged into total blackness. As our pupils battled to adjust to the abrupt change, an image began to form over Hortensia's head.

It was a faint, cloudy image that seemed to ripple through the air. It seemed to shape itself, and then dissolve, and then re-form.

---

* See *The Case of the Vanishing Corpse*

Gradually it became an image something like a man, but unlike any man I had ever seen. It looked a little like a monstrous genie out of Arabian folklore. But more fearsome. More reptilian. A cross between human and crocodile.

This vast, cloudy figure leaned forward over the audience — and we all instinctively shrank back. The head turned, and the eyes glinted, yellow cat-like eyes with vertical pupils, as if he — or it — was studying each one of us.

Then the image opened its mouth as if to speak, and as it did so it flickered and disappeared.

In the same moment that the image vanished, the noises began. Crashing, rumbling explosions, like thunder or underground detonations, echoed around the auditorium at eardrum-bursting level. The entire audience was flinching at each explosion.

Then they stopped.

In the silence I realised that a dim, red light was now surrounding Hortensia on the stage, like some sort of demonic halo. And Hortensia herself began to speak in a strange, strained voice.

'It is I — Tantalus,' she said. 'I have made contact. Open your inner eyes to the cosmic consciousness. You are surrounded by a host of demigods, demons and guardians...'

Many of the audience, I noticed, were glancing nervously around to see if 'his' words were literally true.

'...a host of demigods, demons and guardians who inhabit the inner spaces of your minds. Remember, you are your own godhead...'

Funny, I thought, how this 'Tantalus' spouts the same brand of rubbish as Hortensia!

'...you, yourselves, are gods and kings! Fulfil the destiny of yourself!'

A few minutes later, the lights came up and the show was over.

'Well,' asked Rachel breathlessly, 'what did you think of that?'

'I don't know how they did it,' I replied, 'what trickery or gadgets they used — but they certainly turned on a terrific show.'

CHAPTER 29

'The trouble is,' Rachel remarked, as we walked home from The Inner Temple, 'that I don't understand how they could have done it.'

'It was certainly a very impressive trick,' I admitted.

'You mean the appearance of Tantalus?'

'I mean what looked like the appearance of Tantalus.'

'Any guesses?'

'Well, bear in mind that we were in a very controlled environment. It was their auditorium, set up to achieve the effects they wanted to achieve.'

'And the "Tantalus spirit" is a built-in special-effects trick?'

'Of course it is. You don't really think it could be anything else, do you?'

'Well…could it be a demonic spirit they have conjured up somehow?'

'That appears right on cue? And gives exactly the right performance? I doubt it.'

'So how was it done?' asked Rachel.

'Well…if I was trying to duplicate it I would use a projected movie image.'

'There's a problem with that. In fact, three problems.'

'Such as?'

'First, there was no screen. When the music was

playing, the curtains opened to reveal a large white screen onto which those slides were projected. But when Hortensia started speaking, the curtains closed — and they were still closed when the lights went off and the image appeared. So what was the image projected onto?'

'I don't know. I admit that you can't project a movie image without a screen to project it onto, and I don't know how they worked that one. Second problem?'

'Where did they project it from? The slide projector that was used during the music was sitting in open view on a table in the auditorium. But there was no movie projector in view, was there?'

'No, there wasn't. And I looked around as we were leaving and could see no projection booth. And what's the third problem?'

'The image looked three-dimensional.'

'Yes. It didn't look like your usual two-dimensional movie image.'

'So how did they do that?'

'I don't know how they did any of it. But I'm certain that it is, in principle, all explicable.'

It was a problem we were still talking about as we walked to Philip's house the next morning.

Philip was renting part of an old Roman villa that had been divided up into apartments. His apartment was an L-shaped affair at the front of the building. And being an old villa, it had large rooms and high ceilings. Plenty of room, in fact, for Philip to hold his meetings in.

We arrived just before noon, to find a bunch of people already gathered. As well as Philip himself there was his wife Helen whom we had met briefly at synagogue but never spoken to before. There was a young couple I had seen Philip talking to at synagogue; they were introduced to us as Dan and Elizabeth. And another young couple also rounded up by Philip: Clement and Euodia.

And, of course, there was Cornelius and his family.

His wife's name, I discovered, was Priscilla, and their small son was named Rufus. They were able to tell us that Peter and his companions had already left, heading back to Jerusalem.

'We're all here now,' said Philip, 'let's go in.'

The long dining-room table was set with places for everyone, and a sideboard held a big seafood platter and a huge salad bowl.

'I feel so sad about poor Abigail,' said Rachel later, when we were seated at the table, 'not just because of her horrible death, but because she seems to have been so unhappy.'

'What would you have told her?' I asked Philip, 'if she'd come to you?'

'You answer the question yourself, Ben,' he challenged, 'you should be able to.'

'Thanks, friend!' I said with a laugh.

'Go on, Ben,' chimed in Cornelius, 'I want to hear what you'd say.'

'Alright. Alright. Well...to start with...I think Abigail believed that God is the maker and ruler of the world.'

'Why? Because of her synagogue background?' asked Priscilla.

'More than that. I suspect that everyone — in their heart of hearts — accepts that. Whether they admit it or not.'

'That's a good starting point, honey,' encouraged Rachel, 'keep going.'

'Okay. So what follows from that?' I muttered,

mainly to myself. 'From God is maker it follows that
we are made. We are not a morally vacuous accident
of the natural order, but have the significance of the
"made." What also follows is the notion of purpose.
If we are made, we are made with a purpose.'

'What purpose?' asked young Rufus.

'That's a good question,' I replied patronisingly.

'Then give him a good answer,' laughed Philip.

'In no more than two words!' threw in Cornelius
with a chuckle.

'I'll try,' I muttered, putting my head down to
concentrate. A moment later I said, 'Knowing God.
There — that's two words. How's that?'

'Very good, honey,' said Rachel with delight.

'Don't rest on your laurels, Ben,' urged Cornelius.
'What else would you have told Abigail.'

'That we have lost our purpose. The whole human
race has, I mean. Turned our backs on knowing God.
Rejected God as ruler by running our lives our own
way without him.'

'With what result?' asked Dan.

'Resulting in human nature being corrupted —
corrupted in the direction of being selfish, and thus
in the direction of breaking relationships.'

'Prove it!' challenged Philip.

'Look at human history! Look at any daily newspaper!'

'Good answer. You're getting there, Ben. What
next?'

'God won't put up with human rebellion forever.
If we have our fist in God's face, so to speak, we
must expect God's judgement, condemnation, and
punishment.'

'Isn't that rather harsh? asked Euodia.

'Judgement is God telling us that he takes us

seriously. Our rebellion against our maker (and the subsequent damage we cause) is not ignored or passed over lightly. God is perfectly just and holy as well as perfectly loving.'

'Well, where does his love come into it?' persisted Euodia.

'In what Jesus has done. Jesus called himself "the Good Shepherd who lays down his life for his sheep." When he allowed the authorities to put him to death, Jesus died my death, suffered my punishment, and purchased my forgiveness.'

'But,' interrupted Philip, 'not yours only.'

'Of course not. He died for all his people. The self-sacrifice of Jesus Christ is the biggest love letter in the universe. We are loved more than we can know or imagine. Jesus satisfies God's justice, and shows God's love — both at the same time.'

'And he conquered death,' added Rachel. 'He rose from the grave. I know. I saw him.'

'And that makes him the giver of life,' I continued.

'Define what you mean by "life," ' challenged Philip.

'Well…I think…yes, life, real life, abundant life — eternal life, if you like — means having a personal, positive link with the Living God. A link that makes sense of this life and also survives death.'

'That's what this is all about, isn't it?' asked Dan.

'Yes, it is. The message is one of hope, of a fresh start, of new life in Jesus. But we must respond to that offer. We must turn from our way, to his way. We must stop trusting ourselves and trust him. He must be ruler, not us.'

CHAPTER 30

'You're back!' Momma cried, as we walked in the front door. 'At last you're back. I thought you were never coming home.'

'What's wrong, Momma?' I asked. 'What's happened?'

'What's happened? You ask me what's happened? It's that Mr Jacobson, that's what's happened. He's always ringing up. Ring, ring, ring. Every ten minutes he rings. "Are they back yet?" he asks. What can I say? Can I make you suddenly appear? He says it's urgent. I say what isn't? But still he rings up. Ring, ring, ring. Every ten minutes.'

At the end of this recital Momma collapsed in a chair, pink in the face.

'Well, we're here now,' said Rachel. 'So the next time he rings we'll take the call.'

Sure enough, about a minute and half later the phone began to jangle.

'Bartholomew speaking,' I said, as I picked it up.

'Ben, that you? It's Joe Jacobson here. Where have you been?'

'Never mind where I've been. Where's the fire? What's the emergency?'

'It's Abigail's earrings: they've turned up.'

'Where?'

'In a pawnbroker's shop window. I was walking across town this afternoon on business. I just happened to glance in the window — and there they were!'

'What have you done so far?'

'Nothing. I thought you'd have a better idea than me how this should be tackled.'

'Smart move. Leave it to me. Whereabouts is this place?'

'It's easiest if I take you there. Can you meet me in the Forum in ten minutes?'

'Will do. The Forum in ten minutes. See you there.'

I hung up the phone and turned to Rachel.

'Grab your cloak, sweetheart,' I said. 'We're off again. As one of my noble colleagues would say, the game's afoot!'

'What's this "foot" business?' asked Momma, mopping her pink brow with a tiny lace handkerchief. 'You're living a hand-to-mouth existence and now you're talking about feet. I don't understand.'

'Don't you worry about it, Momma,' said Rachel.

'We have to go out again,' I added.

'Out again already? What if the phone keeps ring, ring, ringing? What do I do? What do I say?'

'It's okay, Momma, Joe Jacobson won't be ringing every ten minutes.'

'You can promise me this?'

'I promise you. We'll be back as soon.'

The Forum is a big place, and as Rachel and I stood on one corner near the pickled herring vendors I realised that I should have been more precise about where we would meet Joe Jacobson.

'There's something fishy about this,' said Rachel.

'Yeah, the pickled herrings,' I replied.

'No, Joe Jacobson. Why hasn't he turned up?'

'Maybe he has. Maybe he's looking for us in the wrong part of the Forum.'

'You didn't set a precise meeting place? Men!' she snorted. 'You shouldn't be allowed out on your own, you really shouldn't!'

'Sorry I'm late,' said a voice behind us. It was Joe. 'I got held up.'

'See,' I said, raising one eyebrow at Rachel, 'just leave it to the men to organise, and there are no problems.'

I didn't hear what she said in reply, but I think it was a snort of derision.

Joe led the way through the late-afternoon shopping crowds, and then plunged into a series of narrow winding alleys on the far side of the Forum.

After five minutes of ducking and weaving our way through narrow, dusty alleys Joe came a halt.

We were facing a shop window. Above it was the sign of the three balls — the trademark of the pawnbroker. Beside the sign was a name: Titus Canby, Licensed Dealer in Second-hand Goods.

Joe led us over to the window and pointed to a pair of silver, star-shaped earrings lying among a jumble of diverse items.

'That's them,' he said, 'that's definitely Rachel's earrings.'

'You're sure?'

'Not a doubt!'

'You stay here, Joe. Rachel and I will go in and investigate.' Then I turned to Rachel and said, 'Would you like a new pair of earrings, darling?'

'Oh, darling! That's exactly what I want,' she replied, catching my meaning at once.

As we pushed open the shop door a small bell

tinkled, and wizened-looking little old Greek man appeared from the back of the shop.

'How can I help you folks?' he said with an oily grin.

'My girlfriend here,' I said, slipping an arm around Rachel's shoulders, 'has fallen in love with those earrings you have in the window.'

'In that case, she's a woman of great discernment and very fine taste, very fine taste indeed. Just a moment and I'll fetch out the earrings in question.'

A moment late he was laying them on the countertop for our inspection.

'Oooo, gorgeous!' squealed Rachel, in a most convincing performance. 'May I try them on?'

'What? And risk you running out of the shop wearing my earrings? Just look at them, young lady, just look at them.'

'What do you want for them?' I asked, having noticed that there were no price tags on any of the goods in the shop.

Titus Canby looked me over carefully, as if estimating my ability to pay.

'For anybody else, 200 shekels. But I like you. You're a nice young couple. And I was in love once myself, many years ago,' (that was hard to believe: this man had never been in love with anything except money!), 'so for you — just 100 shekels. And a real bargain at that price.'

Rachel was gently fingering the earrings, and looking rather solemn.

I knew that she was thinking of the young woman who used to wear them — who had died so violently.

'Do you like them, sweetheart?' I asked softly, prompting her back into the role she was supposed to be playing.

'What? Oh. Oh, yes. I don't just like them, I love them!'

'Wonderful,' said Canby, 'that's settled then — 100 shekels, please.'

'There's just one small problem with that,' I said grimly.

'What problem?' asked Canby nervously.

'These earrings are stolen,' I snapped.

As I spoke, I whipped out my old private investigator's licence and flashed it in front of his eyes — too quickly for him to read, I hoped.

'I'm Officer Quirinius,' I said, 'and this is Officer Junia from the city watch robbery squad.'

'You can't prove anything. Anyway, I'm an honest businessman.'

'You're a receiver of stolen property, Mr Canby, that's what you are.'

'Look, Officer,' said Canby, stepping up close to me, and giving me the full benefit of his breath, which stank of brandy, cheese, and onions, 'this officer really is your girlfriend, isn't she? I can tell just by looking at you two together. What say I just give you the silver earrings and you just go away and forget about it. What do you say, eh?'

'Not enough, Canby,' I snarled, 'not nearly enough!'

'Whadda ya want?' he whined. 'The money outta my safe? You're a bigger crook than I am!'

'Not money, Canby — information.'

'What information?'

'Where did you get the earrings?'

'From a source. I can't give that away. You know that.'

'Tell it to the judge! Looks like we'll have to file an official charge, Officer Junia.'

'No! No! Hold on! I'll tell you, I'll tell you!'

'Tell us then.'

'It was a kid who sold them to me.'

'A kid?'

'Yeah, one of those street urchins. One of those grubby, homeless kids you see living on the streets.'

'Where would a kid get silver earrings like that?'

'Are you joking? You mean the robbery squad doesn't know how the system works?'

'What we know doesn't matter — we want you to tell us!'

'Alright! Alright! The kids are used as runners — as messengers — by the professional thieves. They bring the gear to me, and take the payments back to their masters. That's all I know, honestly.'

'And this particular kid — the one who brought in these earrings — who does he work for?'

'He wasn't one of the regulars. I'd never seen him before. And I ain't seen him since. I don't know who he is, or who he works for.'

Titus Canby was shaking as he spoke. He was terrified, and I believed he was telling the truth.

'Okay,' I said, 'no charges this time. But we will take the earrings with us.'

Rachel and I turned and started for the front door of the shop.

'Hey! Wait!' called out Canby, 'I paid twenty shekels for those earrings — you're not going to leave me out of pocket, are you?'

I pulled twenty shekels out of my toga and dropped them on the counter with a loud rattle. Then we turned and walked out.

As we stepped into the narrow alley in front of the shop Canby's voice came from behind us: 'I only paid ten shekels, but you're not getting any money back!'

With that, the shop door slammed closed, and a heavy bolt could be heard sliding into place.

CHAPTER 31

'Here are Abigail's earrings back,' said Rachel, handing the silver earrings over to Joe Jacobson.

'Thanks,' he said. 'What did you find out?'

'Not a lot,' I admitted. 'But we are getting closer. And the trail is not cold yet.'

'Did you learn anything?' persisted Joe.

'I learned that the earrings did not come from one of Titus Canby's regular suppliers. In other words, they did not come from a professional thief.'

We talked about the significance of this as we walked back to the Forum, where we parted from Joe and headed for home.

I must be honest and admit that at this point I was scratching for information — searching for that one vital clue that would pull together all the pieces of the jigsaw puzzle.

With that in mind, after our evening meal, I told Rachel and Momma that I was going out on a 'scavenger hunt' for scraps of information — planning to call in on Petronius Laconicus at the newspaper, Maximus at the Ipso Vino bar and grill, and Captain Cornelius at his home. Perhaps the journalist, or the bartender, or Cornelius with his city watch connections, could give me some new scrap of information.

What happened after I left I only found out later. So

what I'm telling you now is based on what others told me — and on what I figured out for myself.

When I left, Rachel was feeling at a loose end, her nerves as frayed as mine by the nagging problem of the unsolved mystery.

After the dinner dishes had been washed, wiped and stacked away, she sat at the dining-room table with a scrap of parchment and a quill, doodling away, looking at the problem from every possible angle.

Suddenly, she sat bolt upright and cried out: 'That's it!'

'That's what?' asked Momma, 'What's what? What's it?'

'So...that's what it means,' murmured Rachel, talking to herself. 'And if that's true...then...ah, yes.'

'Rachel, my love,' said Momma, 'don't talk to yourself. It's not healthy. I'm in the room too, you know. You wanna talk? Talk to me.'

'Sorry, Momma. It's just that I'm so preoccupied by this problem. Ben and I both have been. But now I'm beginning to see...'

'Beginning to see what? You start a sentence, finish it. If you start anything you should finish it. That's always a good policy. I used to teach Benjamin when he was a young boy...Hey! Why are you putting on your cloak? Are you going somewhere?'

'Yes, Momma. I'm going. Right now. To check on something.'

'Where? Where are you going?'

'Out.'

'Out? Out? What kind of answer is that? And where is "out"?'

But by then Rachel was down the stairs and was closing the front door behind her.

Rachel hurried through the dark streets of the city.

She pulled her cloak tightly around her, even though it was not a particularly cold night, with a warm, moist breeze blowing in from the Mediterranean.

Caesarea has notoriously bad street-lighting, but enough windows were spilling golden oblongs of light across the streets for Rachel to make her way without stumbling.

Eventually she reached the building. All the main lights were turned off.

'Obviously there's no meeting here tonight,' she muttered to herself.

Up on the first floor one office window was lit up, but she decided to investigate anyway. She might be able to get a look at what she wanted to see, without being seen herself.

She tried the main front door. It was locked. She walked around the building and found a smaller, side door. This too was locked. But she had a plastic credit card in her tunic, and she had learned from me one or two of the disreputable tricks of the trade from my bad old days.

Two minutes of juggling and manipulating with the credit card, and she heard the lock spring open, and felt the door swing inwards.

Stepping inside, Rachel found herself in a long, dark corridor. She eased the door shut behind herself, and then walked slowly, quietly and carefully down the hallway.

She groped her way forward through the dark, with her finger-tips touching the wall and her feet reaching forward cautiously at each step so that she didn't trip or stumble.

After several minutes she reached a large area that was dimly lit. This, she realised, was the main entrance lobby. She had entered it from the rear, and the dim light she could see was the blue–silver moonlight falling through the front windows.

On her left was the main staircase, and Rachel proceeded to climb this, still moving slowly and cautiously. She made sure that her tread was soft, and steadied herself with one hand on the polished timber handrail.

At the top of the stairs was another long, straight corridor. Halfway along, a door was ajar, and yellow light was spilling into the hallway.

Hugging one wall, Rachel crept down the corridor to the open door. She stopped to catch her breath, and then carefully peered around the edge of the door-frame into the room.

There was only one person in the room: a man. She could see the broad expanse of his back as he sat, hunched over his desk, scratching away with a quill.

At that point she must have stumbled, or made a small noise, because the man spun around and called out, 'Who's that? Who's there?'

Rachel stepped forward into the light.

'Oh, it's you,' he said. 'What on earth are you doing here at this time of night?'

'I'm here to accuse you of murder, Lord Weekly,' said Rachel.

'Murder? What murder?' said Weekly, leaning back in his office chair.

'The murder of Abigail Jacobson!'

'That young woman? You're accusing me of murdering her? Why on earth would I do a thing like that?'

'Because she was an intelligent young woman, and she discovered how you work your fraud here at The Inner Temple.'

'Fraud? What fraud? Really, my dear, I haven't the faintest idea what you're talking about.'

'I'm talking about what's in the next room,' said Rachel, 'the room you call your "private meditation chamber." I think the fraud squad would be very interested in the contents of that room. So would the wealthy customers who pay so much money to attend the spectacular seminar shows you turn on here.'

'My dear lady,' said Weekly, his eyelids lowering to a sinister, slit-eyed stare, 'you really pose a serious problem for me. I can't allow you to go around making statements like that, now, can I? You'll only frighten off the punters, and I can't really allow that, now, can I? What did you hope to achieve tonight?'

'I was hoping to get a look at that room without you being here,' admitted Rachel.

'Well, it's too late for that now,' said Weekly.

'In that case, I'm leaving. But my husband Ben and I will be back first thing in the morning with the city watch.'

'No. You're not leaving. You're not going anywhere,' replied Weekly, his voice dropping to a threatening hush.

'Try and stop me!' said Rachel firmly.

'I intend to. Take a look at my right hand. It's a very small automatic pistol I'm holding, but a very deadly one, I do assure you.'

'You wouldn't dare…'

'Oh, but I would dare.'

'You'll never get away with it! How would you dispose of my body? Or explain it away? The corpse of a respectable, law-abiding citizen would be a little difficult to explain.'

'Not at all, my dear, not at all. When I shot you — I will say — I had no idea who you were. All I saw was a shadow at the end of the corridor, and, mistaking you for a thief, I opened fire. Of course, I will explain that I fired only because I saw the glint of the revolver in your hand.'

'But I haven't got a revolver!'

'You will have by the time your body is discovered!'

There was a long silence, while Rachel's mind raced desperately, trying to think of some way out of the deadly situation in which she found herself. When Ben came back home would he wonder where she was? Would he come looking for her? Would he know where to look? She silently cursed herself for not leaving a note explaining where she was going.

Lord Weekly, it appeared, had also been thinking.

'On second thoughts, my dear,' he said, 'I think it might be better if I were not personally involved in your death. And I have thought of a way of arranging that. Turn around and start walking!'

'And if I refuse?'

'Then it's back to Plan A and I shoot you on the spot!'

Rachel turned around and started walking back down the corridor. As soon as she took her first step she felt the sharp jab of the pistol in her back.

'Down the stairs — keep going!' ordered Weekly.

On the ground floor he opened a doorway and pushed Rachel down another flight of stairs. Weekly flicked on the light and Rachel saw that she was in a cellar, with barrels of beer and wine, and cases full of bottles stacked around the walls.

'Stand still, with your hands behind your back,' growled Weekly.

Rachel did as she was told, and shortly felt a rope being slipped around her wrists and pulled tight.

'Now, move — over to that far wall!'

There was a steep ramp against the far wall, and at the foot of the ramp, a mattress leaning against a bale of hay. Weekly pulled the hay and the mattress to one side.

'Lie down there, at the foot of the ramp,' ordered the murderer.

Rachel, her mind still racing in desperation, did as she was told.

'In the morning,' explained Weekly, 'very early — just after dawn — that trap-door up there will open, and a heavy barrel of wine will be rolled down. But instead of it coming to rest against the mattress and hay bale, as it usually does, the full force of its weight will hit your slender body, my dear. You will be crushed to death. Medically speaking, I imagine that you will die from massive internal injuries.'

'How will you explain that?'

'You are a thief — obviously. You stole into the cellar in the dead of night, intending to steal our liquor supplies, but found yourself trapped, and fell asleep (most unfortunately) at the foot of the ramp.'

'But the ropes on my hands and feet — how will you explain those?'

'There will be no ropes to explain.'

'But the minute you take the ropes off I will move out of the way. I won't just lie here,' said Rachel defiantly, 'I can promise you that.'

'Oh yes, you will! You will lie there sleeping like a baby.'

Rachel saw that Weekly was holding a large, wicked-looking hypodermic needle in his hand. A moment later the needle plunged into her arm.

As she was falling asleep Rachel could feel the ropes being loosened and removed.

CHAPTER 32

'How was your expedition, Benjamin?' asked Momma, as I bounded up the stairs. 'Did you find out anything?'

'Not a thing,' I replied. 'It was a complete washout.'

I went into the kitchen and put on the coffee, then I came back to ask, 'Where's Rachel? Has she gone to bed?'

'She's out. That's where she is,' explained Momma.

'Where "out"?'

'Just "out." That's all she told me when she rushed off down the stairs.'

'When was this?'

'Three hours ago. Maybe three and half.'

'Three hours! And there's been no word from her? She didn't telephone?'

'I've just been sitting here, all by myself,' said Momma, 'listening to the clock tick.'

'Did she give you any hint, any clue, as to where she might be going?'

'Not a sausage,' said Momma, 'not a word.'

'Did she say why she was going?'

'Not even that. She sat at that table, doodling on a scrap of parchment, when suddenly she jumped up and said something about "that's what it means," and then she said she was going out. That's all.'

I sat down at the dining-room table where Rachel had been sitting. The scrap of parchment with Rachel's doodles on it was still there.

She had drawn a sketch of Abigail's earrings. A very accurate, life-size sketch. And underneath she had scrawled: 'six not seven.'

Now, what did that mean: six not seven?

Six not seven? I didn't understand.

Six not seven?

Of course! That's what it meant! Clever Rachel. I should have seen it for myself. Six not seven. That explained a great deal.

And that was where Rachel had gone.

I grabbed the telephone.

'Come on — answer, answer,' I muttered to myself, while the phone at the other end jangled.

'Hello?' said a sleepy voice at the other end eventually.

'Cornelius? It's me — Ben. Rachel's in trouble. I need your help.'

'Trouble? What sort of trouble?'

'Listen — she solved the mystery of Abigail's death, and then set off on her own to do something about it. She's been gone for over three hours. I'm worried, Cornelius.'

'What can I do to help?'

'Can you get a patrol of your soldiers together, and meet me in front of The Inner Temple?'

'I can have them there in half an hour.'

'Make it fifteen minutes! I'll see you there.'

I went to the bookshelf where I kept my old revolver, loaded it, and stuck it in my belt.

'I'm going, Momma,' I said. 'Rachel needs help.'

'You be careful, Benjamin my boy. I worry about you. And you bring Rachel back safe and sound.'

'I intend to,' I said grimly, 'or die trying.'

I hurried downstairs, locked the front door behind me, and ran to the end of the street. There, on the corner, I hailed a passing cab.

'The Inner Temple,' I told the cab-driver, 'and I'll pay you twice what the meter says if you get me there in ten minutes.'

As the cab flew through the darkened streets of the sleeping city my mind flew through the mystery we had been wrestling with.

Those words of Rachel's — 'six not seven' — were the key that pulled the whole jigsaw puzzle together. I now knew *where* Abigail had been murdered — but who had killed her? As the pieces of the puzzle turned over in my mind the answer to that 'who' question also became clear. As did the motive.

By the time the cab pulled up in front of The Inner Temple I knew everything.

As the cab pulled away again I tried the front doors. They were locked. But they were also glass, and I didn't have time for the niceties.

Using the butt of my revolver I smashed a pane of glass, reached inside, released the lock, and opened the door.

The vast lobby was deserted, and looked quite ghostly, lit only by the pale moonlight.

I stood in the middle of the lobby and bellowed at the top of my lungs: 'Rachel! Rachel! Can you hear me?'

Silence was the only reply. Silence broken only by the echo of my own voice.

I prowled around the lobby for a minute or two, looking for some sign of Rachel's presence. As I reached the main staircase I became aware of a shadowy figure creeping cautiously down the stairs.

'Who is that doing all that shouting?' said the shadow. 'Clear off or I'll call the city watch.'

It was Lord Weekly — just the man I wanted to see!

'I've already done that,' I explained. 'They're on their way.'

'Who are you? And what's the meaning of all this?'

'Ben Bartholomew is the name. You haven't forgotten me, Lord Weekly, I'm sure of that. My wife was here earlier tonight. And I want to know what you've done with her!'

'Your wife? My dear chap, you're sadly mistaken. Your good lady wife has been nowhere near this place tonight — I know, I've been here all night working late on the accounts.'

'You're lying, Weekly! I know you're lying! Lead the way upstairs to your office — we'll start the search there.'

'Now listen here, dear chap. You really must restrain yourself. I am telling you the absolute and simple truth.'

'This is a revolver in my hand, Weekly. A large-calibre revolver. If I pulled the trigger, there wouldn't be much of you left to argue. Now — upstairs to your office, you lead the way.'

'If you insist, dear chap, if you insist. But you are making a serious mistake.'

When we reached the office I made Weekly stand against the wall, feet apart, while I searched the room. No sign of Rachel.

'Where is she?' I growled.

'I don't know what this bee in your bonnet is,' whined Weekly, 'but I haven't the faintest idea where your wife is.'

'If you don't tell me the truth,' I said, quietly and menacingly, 'I'll beat it out of you.'

'No need to do that, Ben,' said a voice from the doorway.

It was Cornelius.

'The forces of law and order have arrived,' he said.

'Oh, thank goodness for that,' gasped Weekly, 'this madman has been threatening me! I want him placed under arrest immediately.'

'Any sign of Rachel yet, Ben?' said Cornelius, ignoring Weekly.

'Not yet. I'm sure he knows where she is,' I explained, 'but he's not talking.'

'Well, don't worry. My men will take this place apart. We'll find her. Meanwhile, what do we do with Lord Weekly?'

'This is the man,' I explained, 'who murdered Abigail Jacobson.'

'Captain,' spluttered Weekly, 'you're not going to believe these outrageous accusations, are you? This Bartholomew man has gone mad — stark, staring mad!'

'Lord Weekly,' said Cornelius in reply, 'you are hereby charged with the murder of Abigail Jacobson. You don't have to say anything, but anything you do say may be taken down in writing and used in evidence against you. Trooper, handcuff this man and hold him in the lobby until he's wanted for further questioning.'

'I'll sue you for false arrest,' screamed Weekly, as he was dragged away. 'Wrongful arrest and criminal defamation! You'll hear from my lawyers!'

'Now, Ben,' said Cornelius, 'where do we start?'

'She could be anywhere. We'll have to search the whole building,' I explained.

'Leave it to me,' snapped the Captain, as he began to give orders to the patrol he'd brought with him.

Over the early morning hours that followed, The Inner Temple was turned upside-down. All of the offices were searched, and all of the store rooms. The bar, the lobby, the main auditorium, the 'backstage' area behind the auditorium — everywhere.

A number of interesting discoveries were made. For instance, in a hidden drawer in Weekly's office a second set of accounts books were found. So, presumably, on top of everything else, Weekly was cheating on his tax. And in the ceiling above the stage we found a machine for manufacturing clouds of 'dry ice' — thick, white clouds of carbon dioxide. Obviously part of the special-effects machinery built into the auditorium. But there was no sign of Rachel.

It was dawn, and there was a grey, early morning light coming in through the windows when we all assembled in the lobby to assess what we had covered. Weekly was there, slumped in a chair and looking miserable.

'We've done everything, Ben,' said Cornelius, 'there's nowhere left to look.'

'There *must* be! There *must* be!' I said, prowling restlessly around the perimeter of the lobby as I spoke.

'What's this?'

What I was pointing at was a door that was covered in the same wallpaper that covered the main walls of the lobby. The effect was to make it almost invisible.

'Has anyone tried this door?' I asked.

The troopers all shook their heads in response.

I tried the door. It was not locked, and swung inwards as soon as I turned the handle.

'It's the wine cellar,' I said, as I reached inside, turned on the light, and started down the narrow cellar stairs.

Then I saw her!

'Rachel!' I called out. But she didn't move! She was lying on the floor, at the foot of a steep ramp. Her eyes were closed.

I hurried to her side.

'Rachel! Rachel! Speak to me! Speak to me!'

I rubbed her wrists and lifted up her head. Slowly her eyes began to open.

'Ben...' she said feebly.

As she spoke, a crack of sunlight lit up the floor where she lay. I looked over my shoulder and saw that a trap door had been opened.

I placed my hands under Rachel's shoulders and, slowly and gently began to move her. As I did so a noise came from the trap-door above. I took Rachel in my arms and lifted her up. Then I turned to carry her up to the lobby. At that moment came the thunder of timber rolling over timber. I turned around in time to see a giant wine barrel come flying down the ramp and shatter on the concrete floor where, not a moment before, Rachel had been lying.

CHAPTER 33

There were five of us in Lord Weekly's office: Cornelius, Rachel and myself were standing around the desk, while Weekly was slumped glumly in a chair — still handcuffed — and an officer was standing behind Cornelius taking notes.

'Are you sure you're up to this, Rachel?' asked Cornelius.

'It took three cups of coffee and a long hug from Ben,' she replied, 'but I'm fine now.'

'She's a tough cookie,' I said with pride.

'Okay then — what's all this about?' asked Cornelius.

'Rachel is the one who discovered the key to the case,' I replied, 'the credit goes to her. On Abigail's original list of temples there were seven names, and we took them to be seven different temples. However, the first six names are lined up in a neat column while the seventh name is slightly indented. That should have given us the clue in the first place.'

'The clue to what?' asked Cornelius.

'It should have told us,' said Rachel, 'that the last name was not another temple but a comment on the one above. The Haunted Temple was Abigail's nickname, or private label, for The Inner Temple.'

'You mean that...?' said Cornelius.

'That's right,' I said, 'there never was any mysterious Haunted Temple — this place is the "haunted temple!" Rachel spotted that. She doodled a note to herself saying "six not seven" — meaning that there were only six temples on Abigail's list, not seven.'

'The implication of that being...what exactly?'

'If this was the last temple that Abigail visited, then quite possibly this is where she died. But why? Well, this is the most clearly fraudulent of all the temples and Abigail was a bright young woman. If she had discovered how the fraud was worked, that might have been motive enough to kill her.'

'I see. So, how *did* the fraud work?' asked Cornelius.

'These rooms — all the rooms opening off this corridor — should all be the same size,' said Rachel. Then she turned to me and added, 'You explain, I'm feeling tired.'

'When we first walked along this corridor we noticed that all the doors were exactly the same distance apart,' I said, as Rachel sank into a padded leather armchair in a corner of the office. 'But when we entered this office and looked through that connecting door, the next office looked much smaller — and curtain-lined. Logically, the office next door to this one *is* the same size, and the curtains we can see through the connecting door are there to hide what it contains.'

'I see. Or, I think I see.'

'On top of which, Weekly called it his "private meditation room." Now, he's the money man of this operation, the Marketing Manager — does he strike you as the type to have a "private meditation room"?'

'Probably not,' admitted Cornelius.

'That suggested that Weekly's so-called "private meditation room" was really the hidden projection booth used to produce the image of the spirit Tantalus at Hortensia's seances. After all, these rooms all overlook the auditorium, and a movie image could easily be projected from here.'

'One thing I still don't know,' said Rachel, 'is what the movie image was projected onto.'

'Onto a cloud of thick, white carbon dioxide gas — produced from 'dry ice'. We found the machinery for doing so above the stage.'

'And that explains,' she said, 'why the image appeared to writhe and shiver in a three-dimensional way.'

'Exactly.'

'And that's why,' added Cornelius, 'when we searched that room we found a movie projector and all those metal film cans.'

'I think I understand it all now,' said Rachel thoughtfully. 'While Hortensia lectured, the lights in the auditorium were turned up, so that the eyes of everyone in the audience would be adjusted to bright light. Then, at the climax, the audience was suddenly plunged into pitch darkness, under cover of which a cloud of thick white gas was released from above the stage, and that strange movie image of Tantalus projected onto the cloud. Then before the audience could tumble to what was going on, the projected image stopped, and loud, unsettling thunder and explosive sounds were played through the quadrophonic speakers into the auditorium. The whole effect being both disturbing and spectacular.'

'Just so,' I said. 'Abigail uncovered the fraud. That's why she was murdered. But who killed her? When I thought about it, I realised that Weekly had given himself away. When we first spoke to him he said how sad it was for a nice young girl like that to be found dead in a ditch. But we hadn't told him where the body was found, and it hadn't been in the papers. So how could he know? Unless he put her there himself.'

'Condemned out of his own mouth?' asked Cornelius.

'Yes. And there was more,' I added. 'The strange semi-circular shape of the wound that crushed Abigail's skull: I think you'll find it exactly matches the size and shape of those metal film cans next door. What happened, Weekly? Did she walk in while you were working the movie projector and threaten to expose you? And did you, in a panic, hit her over the head with the nearest weapon to hand — a heavy metal film can?'

Lord Weekly did not respond. He just sat in his chair, sunk in self-pity.

'Then there was the matter of the earrings,' I continued. 'I had been trying to work out what was different between Hortensia's appearance the first time we saw her and the second time. Then I remembered: the first time she had been wearing sparkling silver earrings that caught the light. The second time, they were gone. It was foolish of you to give her those earrings in the first place, Weekly.'

'I didn't give them to her,' muttered Weekly. 'She saw them on my desk and asked for them. She's like that.'

'Did she know about the murder?' asked Cornelius.

'No. No, she knew nothing,' said Weekly. 'She just saw the earrings on my desk and wanted them. So I gave them to her. But after these two came here investigating, I got worried that the earrings might give me away. So I stole them from Hortensia's dressing table and disposed of them.'

'But even then,' I said, 'you couldn't resist making some money out of them. Instead of throwing them into the harbour, you sold them to a pawnbroker.'

'One thing I still don't understand,' said Rachel, 'is the role of Vacuus in all of this. Was he involved? And why was he killed?'

'Yes, he was most certainly involved, sweetheart,' I explained. 'When I thought about it, I realised that several things gave him away. For a start, in my first conversation with him I referred to Abigail only as "Jacobson" — but later in that same conversation he called her "Abigail Jacobson." How did he know? Because he was involved! Also, for a man who was supposed to know everything about the temples of Caesarea, why did he not tell me that The Inner Temple was a fraud? Because he was working for The Inner Temple at the time! And why did he laugh when I suggested he might help me? Because he knew that he had been hired to threaten us, and frighten us off the investigation!'

'So it was Vacuus who did all those things to us?' said Rachel.

'Yes, it was. Remember, he was by profession a thug.'

'But why was he then killed?' asked Cornelius.

'Probably because he knew too much and decided to try a little blackmail on his own account. Was he the person you used to carry the body of Abigail outside the city limits and dump it?' I asked, turning to Weekly. 'And did the denarius finally drop — even in his slow brain — that what you were guilty of was murder, and you could therefore be blackmailed? Is that what happened? And then to shut him up, you murdered him too, didn't you, Weekly?'

By now that distinguished nobleman Lord Weekly

was tired of denial, or, perhaps, just plain tired, because he nodded his head in silent confession.

'I'll need to get all this typed up into a report,' said Cornelius. 'You two have done a great job.'

'But only in the nick of time,' I said ruefully.

'A nick will do,' said Rachel, 'as long as it is in time!'

As Cornelius and the officer led Weekly away, Rachel asked, 'Will Hortensia be arrested too?'

'For what?'

'For being part of the fraud, of course.'

'I'm not sure she was part of the fraud.'

'What on earth do you mean?'

'I mean that she's not a very down-to-earth person. She's strictly off with the pixies, and Lord Weekly could have been running the spirit-faking business without her knowing anything about it.'

'Do you really think that's possible?'

At that moment Hortensia herself came sweeping dramatically into the room.

'I've just been told,' she announced loudly. 'Poor Arthur. I'm sure he thought that what he was doing was for the best. But it was quite unnecessary. He should just have left it up to me, and not tried to ice the cake.'

'"Poor Arthur?" Surely it should be "Poor Abigail?"' I suggested.

'Oh, yes. Her too,' said Hortensia, in her grand manner. 'I find it most distressing that Arthur was projecting movies of Tantalus when all the time I thought I was summoning him up. Where do you think I went wrong? Was it my meditation technique?'

Still muttering questions to herself, Hortensia

swept back out of the room as dramatically as she had entered it.

'A true believer?' asked Rachel.

'Yes, a true believer,' I said. 'But what she believes in — her "world view" — is false.'

'But how can she be so unmoved by the tragedy of what has happened?'

'When you are a "god," other people are not likely to matter very much to you.'

'I suppose so. Much better to give up this silly nonsense of being our own "gods" and to live under the direction of the God Who is There.'

'Yes, to have a personal, positive link...' I added.

'...through Jesus,' completed Rachel, getting up out of the armchair.

As she stepped to my side I slipped an arm around her shoulder and said, 'Time to go home, my love. Time to go home.'

YOUR QUEST FOR TRUTH

WHAT IS A "WORLD VIEW"?
All human beings hold some 'world view' or other.

Not just philosophers, but poets and pastry-cooks, scientists and shop-assistants, technicians and truck-drivers — everyone has a 'world view.'

What is a 'world view?' It is, if you like, a kind of mental map of reality. A picture that we hold inside our heads of what really exists, of what the world is like, and how it works.

Our world view is how we think about ourselves, other people, the natural world, and God (or ultimate reality).

A CHOICE OF WORLD VIEWS
In this book I have sketched very briefly (and in parody form) a number of popular world views. They are as follows:

1. *Theism* (in the synagogue) A basic belief in God as the self-revealing creator and ruler of the universe.
2. *Deism* (in **The Temple of the Great Clockmaker**) The belief in a hidden God who lives entirely apart from our world and does not influence the lives of human beings nor the day-to-day working of the universe. (Today, people holding this view usually call themselves 'agnostics'.)
3. *Materialism* (in *The Temple that Matters*) The belief that nothing exists but matter and its movements and modifications. It includes a tendency to believe that whatever happens is determined by cause and effect; and a tendency to prefer, and to value highly, material possessions and physical comforts.

4. *Nihilism* (in **The Nothingness Temple**) The total rejection and denial of all traditional value statements and moral judgements based on the belief that there is no objective basis for truth, meaning, morality or beauty.

5. *Existentialism* (in **The Temple of the Golden Eye**) A set of beliefs stressing the importance of existence, or being, as such (because, it says, the universe is absurd and alienating). It asserts that people make themselves what they are — but that they must do so in ignorance of the future, and be aware that life terminates in nothingness.

6. *Pantheism* (in **The One Temple**) The belief that the divine is all-inclusive, and that individual people and the material universe are just manifestations of a transcendent reality. It thereby denies the importance of personality, and identifies God with the universe.

7. *The New Age* (in **The Inner Temple**) A popular mixture of mysticism, metaphysics, astrology, spiritualism, holism and occultism.

8. *Biblical Christianity* (in the meeting at Philip's home) Belief in God as creator and ruler of the universe who reveals himself through a person and a book — through Jesus and the Bible. It includes the belief that through Jesus it is possible for us to have a personal, positive link with the Living God.

I make no secret of the fact that, for me, Christianity is the only world view that passes the most stringent truth value tests.

YOU: THE PHILOSOPHER
Have you ever stopped to think what world view, what picture of reality, exists inside your head?

Have you ever asked yourself what assumptions or pre-suppositions you hold about the basic make-up of the world?

To discover the world view that lies at the back of your mind, ask yourself these questions:

1. *What do I believe to be the nature of external reality, that is, the world around us?* Is it chaos? Or order? Is it the result of an accident? Or does it exist for a purpose?
2. *What do I believe a human being to be?* A complex machine? An animal? The image of God?
3. *What do I believe happens to a person at death?* Is it just the end? Or is it a transformation? Is it a new beginning? Or a judgement?
4. *How do I know what is right and wrong?* Is morality a human invention? Or just what is useful for survival? Or is morality as eternal as God?
5. *What do I think is the meaning of human history?* Is it going anywhere? Is there a purpose and direction? Or is it a meaningless muddle?

You might find it a worthwhile exercise to take a sheet of paper and write down your answers. This list of questions (modified from a list in James Sire's excellent book *The Universe Next Door*) will help you to understand the world view that is working away inside your head at this very moment!

MAKING THE CHOICE
Sometimes, we absorb our world view uncritically (from our parents, or influential friends or teachers, or the media), without thinking it through for ourselves.

So, how can we do that? How can we critically examine a world view?

Here are four truth value tests (again adapted from James Sire's book) which, taken together, will help you to evaluate intelligently any world view.

1. The 'Does-it-fit-together?' or Coherence Test

Every world view contains a whole swag of assumptions. And we tend to be more interested in the conclusions, or implications, of a world view than its underlying assumptions.

For that reason, it is an excellent test to dig out the unexamined assumptions that underlie a world view and examine them — particularly to see whether any of them contradict one another.

Biblical Christianity passes this test with flying colours. There is a central core of teaching to which the whole of the Bible relates. This core is called the 'gospel,' meaning 'good news.'

Once you understand that core teaching, you will see exactly how consistent and coherent the Bible is. How well, in other words, it all fits together.

There are many excellent books that summarise this core: *A Fresh Start* by John Chapman and *Basic Christianity* by John Stott are two of the best. If you would like to see this core applied to the whole Bible, read *According to Plan* by Graham Goldsworthy.

2. The 'Does-it-fit-the-facts?' or Correspondence Test

A world view can be discarded if it fails to correspond to the plain facts of the world.

There are points at which every world view can be tested in this regard. How well does it fit what we know about human nature? The universe? Morality? History?

The Biblical view of human nature, it seems to me, is the only one that really fits the facts as we know them.

The Bible says that human nature is not simply good, as the humanists say, nor simply bad, as the pessimists say, but rather a good thing gone bad. The Bible's view of human nature tells us why humans can be both creative and destructive, both cruel and kind. We are made, says the Bible, in the image of the Living God, but our nature is scarred by our rebellion against the God who made us.

And all of us rebel against God — usually by simply ignoring him.

The facts of history, too, support what the Bible says. To check this out read *The Truth About Jesus* by Paul Barnett.

Some people are troubled by the Bible's claim that Jesus came back from the dead. But once again there is solid historical evidence. You'll find it summarised in *Who Moved the Stone?* by Frank Morrison, in my detective novel *The Case of the Vanishing Corpse*, and in Paul Barnett's book mentioned above.

3. The 'Does-it-explain-what-it-claims-to-explain?' Test

Some world views claim to be able to explain, for example, why human beings are moral creatures — but on close examination their explanations fail.

Moral values and facts are two different things. I would claim that all world views, except Biblical Christianity, have difficulty establishing a foundation for morality. Moral values, in the end, come from

God, and world views that reject God lose the foundations of morality.

This test applies in other areas too.

For instance, science can explain (up to a point, at least) *how* the world was created, but not *who* created it and *why*. That's why scientific materialism can never be, on its own, a fully satisfactory world view. Biblical Christianity, on the other hand, rests upon the self-revelation of the Living God: and who knows more than God?

Questions such as these are examined in a book called *The God Who is There* by Francis Schaeffer.

4. The 'Does-it-satisfy-my-personal-needs?' Test

I put this test last because it is the most unreliable of the lot. On the other hand, it is not unimportant.

You'll find information about how Biblical Christianity passes this test in such autobiographies as *Joni* by Joni Erickson, and *Born Again* by Chuck Colson.

In the end, you can only apply this test to a world view from the inside. It is only when you turn from your way to God's way, only when you submit to Jesus, that it all makes personal and satisfying sense. (I deal with this in my detective novel *The Case of the Secret Assassin*.)

Biblical Christianity is not based (as other world views are) in the self, or the universe, but in the Living God who transcends all: the infinite-personal God in whom all reason, all goodness, all truth, all love, and all reality find their origins.